For The Love Of You

Pacific Vista Ranch

BOOK THREE

CLAIRE MARTI

FOR THE LOVE OF YOU
Pacific Vista Ranch, Book 3
Copyright © 2020 by Claire Marti

E-Book: 978-1-7333046-4-1
Print: 978-1-7333046-5-8

This is a work of fiction. Names, characters, places and incidents are either the product of the author's imagination or are used fictitiously, and any resemblance to actual persons, living or dead, business establishments, events or locales is entirely coincidental.

Printed in the USA.

Cover Design and Interior Format

DEDICATION

To my papa—the original French soccer star.

ACKNOWLEDGEMENTS

WRITING THIS BOOK WAS A smoother ride than the last one! I loved being able to write about a French hero because I'm half-French and my time in France growing up is an integral part of who I am.

I'm grateful for all the assistance I received. Without all the input and support, I couldn't have done it! Thank you Cynthia St. Aubin for your artistic insights, Kerrigan Byrne for always listening, Anna Bradley for all the venting, Liana de La Rosa for your excellent blurb skills, and Priya Huggett for the professional athlete contract information. I want to thank my wonderful beta readers and critique partners: Kay Bennett, Joanna Kelly, Leslie Hachtel, and April Fink—you each help me more than you could imagine. I appreciate your time and opinions.

To my wonderful editor, Lindsey Faber, thank you for your keen insight and your brilliant ideas in bringing Dylan and Gabriel's story to life. To my brother Robert Petretti–thanks for your love and support, both as my big brother and as proofreader extraordinaire.

Last but not least, to Todd for being my very own hero. I love you. And, finally to my furry kids: Lola, Beau and Josie, thanks for providing me daily laughs and all the cuddles.

PROLOGUE

Last Summer

DYLAN MCNEILL TOSSED HER SMART-PHONE across the room, not caring if it shattered against the centuries-old white plaster walls of her best friend Lily's Parisian flat. She'd *known*. She'd known *and* she'd informed her family on more than one occasion.

When her father shared the shocking news he'd agreed to allow an old Hollywood director buddy film a large-scale Western on their secluded horse-breeding ranch, she'd *known* the paparazzi would resurrect the McNeill tragedy.

Unable and unwilling to watch her beloved Pacific Vista Ranch be overrun with a movie crew and be forced to relive the painful past, she'd fled to Paris. In France, she could stay with her art school friend, focus on painting, and yes, play ostrich with her head buried in the sand until filming finished. While her sisters Sam and Amanda both worked with horses on the ranch, Dylan could paint anywhere. So she'd run.

She'd *known* and her intuition was one-hundred-percent correct. Why did being right bring no relief? Now all the online tabloids trumpeted the twelve-year-old story of her mother's tragic death once again, complete with all the unfounded vicious rumors and nasty insinuations.

Memories of helicopters swarming above and paparazzi stalking on the ground below slammed into her, stealing her breath and twisting her gut. Just as agonizing as the day her family's life altered forever. The day she'd lost her mother.

Distraught, she tossed on her shortest dress and steepest stilettos and recruited her loyal friend Lily. Desperate to avoid the news, she high-tailed it to the closest nightclub to drink champagne and dance her turbulent emotions out of her system.

Lily hit the dance floor and Dylan sipped—well, actually swigged if she was being honest—her second glass of champagne. Then, she inhaled the most delicious aroma, somehow both tart and spicy. When she turned her head to see if the visual lived up to the scent, her breath lodged in her throat.

Dark hair cut short emphasized the shape of his head, but was long enough on top to tousle with her hands. Her fingers tingled, torn between wanting to paint him and wanting to run her fingers through his hair and discover if it was as silky as it looked. His perfect profile belonged in bronze, suitable to grace an old Roman coin. Sculpted jaw, straight nose, chiseled cheekbones, and firm lips quirked into a smile. His arm resting on the black shiny bar rippled with sinewy muscle.

The stranger turned his head and flashed white teeth in a confident grin, addressing her in French. "Like what you see?"

Something about him looked familiar, but she didn't bother to search her brain for details.

She nodded and returned his cocky smile. "You're beautiful. Is your dance card full or would you like to dance with me?"

"Vous ete Américaine?" Even in the dim lighting of the smoky club, his bottle green eyes gleamed with interest.

"Oui. Je m'appelle Dylan. Voulez-vous danser?" So much for her excellent French accent.

He pivoted from the bar with a fluid grace usually reserved for dancers or athletes and grabbed her hand. Every nerve ending in her body ignited and when he pulled her against his lean, muscular body and began to sway to the tempo of the pumping club music, she wove her arms around his neck and indulged herself by raking her fingers through his thick hair. He growled low in his throat and captured her lips in a deep kiss. Passion flared and a moan escaped her. He tasted as delicious as he smelled–tart, sweet, and a little mysterious.

He murmured an invitation against her mouth and unable to resist the potency of him, she deepened the kiss and melted against him. Here was a true escape. The only thoughts registering in her brain now were how fast could they get out of this bar and continue this dance alone together.

Suddenly, all she craved was this man.
This man would help her feel.
This man would help her forget.

CHAPTER 1

Current Day

DYLAN MCNEILL PRESSED BOTH HANDS against her churning belly, willing the whipping butterfly wings to subside. Why had she thought it would be a good idea to accept celebrity soccer legend Gabriel DuVernay's invitation to attend his first home game with the Los Angeles Galaxy soccer team?

Now she stood a few feet away from the private entrance to the stadium's VIP lounge and cursed her rash decision. When she'd stolen out of his Paris apartment at dawn last summer, she hadn't figured on seeing him again, especially because she'd disappeared without saying goodbye.

Not that she could avoid seeing him splashed online and on magazine covers–usually with the supermodel du jour plastered against his Greek-god body. The press loved Gabriel for his ability to score with beautiful women almost as much as for his world record-breaking goals on the field.

After all, the passionate night they'd shared now seemed like a vivid dream, almost too incredible to happen more than once. Lightning didn't strike twice, right? Yet here she was. Despite the niggling doubt about opening herself up to unwelcome publicity.

"Are you coming in or waiting for someone?" A mountain of a man in a security guard uniform demanded.

Dylan handed him the VIP pass Gabriel had overnighted to her. Although he'd offered her two tickets for the game, she'd chosen to come alone. Her sisters and friends would have asked too many questions and she'd wanted—no, needed—to see Gabriel one on one. She owed him an overdue apology.

The guard waved her toward the double-door entrance marked Sky Box. Another hulking guy in black opened the locked door and gestured for her to enter. Floor-to-ceiling windows dominated the far wall, giving an unobstructed view of the arena; trays heaped with colorful appetizers covered modern high-top white tables with silver legs. About twenty well-dressed men and women were sipping cocktails and chatting, with most focused on the action below.

A few people glanced over at her curiously, and then returned their attention to the field. Dylan smoothed back a strand of her long hair she'd carefully styled into casual beachy waves. The last time she'd seen Gabriel, she'd looked like Medusa with her tangled après-sex hair.

A pretty blonde bartender in a starched white blouse poured her a flute of Veuve Cliquot. The crispness of the bubbles bursting on her tongue reminded her of what she'd been drinking when she'd first met Gabriel that steamy evening in Paris. *And experienced the first, best, and only one-night stand of my life.*

She strolled over to an empty seat, set down her daffodil-colored clutch, and searched the field. Instantly, she spotted Gabriel—his stride was long and smooth, his muscular legs pumping with the grace of a cheetah. A powerful creature who always procured his prey and hit his target. He'd scored more goals in his career than anyone since Brazilian soccer god Pelé, back in the last century. Sweat gleamed on his tawny skin, but somehow Gabriel made it all look natural and effortless, like he'd exited the womb with the black and white ball.

Maybe he had. She shivered, the visceral memory of all the varied beautiful ways he moved off the field rushing through her. Their physical chemistry was magical, but they'd also spent the evening sharing intimate conversation. He'd been a sunny respite during one of the blackest moments of her life. Maybe if she hadn't been desperate to check in with her twin sister at home, she would have stayed until morning.

Because she occasionally followed—oh, who was she kidding? Because she diligently tracked Gabriel online, she'd recently learned he had signed an astronomical nine-figure contract with the L.A. Galaxy. It even eclipsed the one David Beckham received back in the day. When she realized the most fascinating man she'd ever met would be living in Southern California, a chill had shot down her spine. Was it fate?

Since she'd seen him last, casual dating had lost its appeal. She'd buried herself in her art studio and poured all her emotions onto her canvases. Now she was the only single McNeill sister, what with Sam married to the love of her life and Amanda's engagement party fast approaching at the end of the month. Unlike her sisters, who'd found their dream careers early on their family's horse-breeding ranch, Dylan still hadn't broken out in the art world.

Not that she felt like a loser or anything. Nope, not at all.

But until her family and the world recognized her painting as her career, not just a hobby, she refused to rest. And she refused to trade on her family's famous name. She'd chosen to paint as Dylan Marie because the McNeills had already suffered enough at the hands of the paparazzi–no need to attract additional attention.

Applause and shouts erupted across the arena, jolting Dylan from her reminiscing and the slippery slope toward self-pity. She leapt to her feet just in time to see Gabriel score the winning goal. The excitement was infectious and she cheered and high-fived the couple bouncing up and down next to her. Anticipation thrummed through her veins.

After the on-field celebrations ended and the players streamed off the field, her phone beeped.

Can't wait to see you. I'll be up in 10. Gabriel.

A shiver of excitement trickled down her spine. She swallowed the burst of nerves and touched up her pale pink lipstick. Would the present day Gabriel live up to her memories from the most incredible night of her life?

After a quick shower to rinse off the sweat from the exhilarating match, Gabriel threw on a black t-shirt and faded jeans and sauntered up the back stairs to join Dylan. When he reached the suite entrance, the adrenaline rush from the game still coursed through his veins. Seeing Dylan again meant his day could only soar higher. No woman he'd met compared to the fiery beauty.

The last time he'd seen her, her sexy body had been curled up in his arms in his Paris apartment. They'd talked until 3 a.m. and while sharing a baguette, some Brie, and one of his family's Burgundies, he'd learned she was an artist from California. When they'd fallen asleep together, her auburn hair had spread along his dark sheets like a silken blanket of autumn leaves.

In the morning, he'd woken and reached for her, but the pillow had been cool. Even though he'd had an early flight for a match in Munich, he'd wanted more time with her. Time for a long steamy shower and a shared café au lait at least.

Women didn't usually leave him before morn-ing. Actually, women *never* left without saying goodbye. Dylan was different. She'd intrigued him with her excellent French, her sparkling chocolate brown eyes, and her confidence. No avaricious gleam in her gaze or even any recognition. She hadn't been one of the football groupies, looking for five minutes of fame. Over the last year, he'd seen her face in the news, only to learn she was the daughter of Hollywood royalty and shunned the spotlight. She'd grown up under its glare in America.

He'd been unable to forget her and the opportunity to play soccer in California offered a silver lining–seeing Dylan McNeill again. And now he was ready to discover if they'd have a second chance for a morning after. If Dylan accompanied him back to his place in Manhattan Beach tonight, his day would be pretty damn perfect.

Hell, his life would be pretty damn perfect.

When he pushed open the door, his gaze honed in on her fiery mane, which cascaded down her slender back. She turned her head and a slow smile spread across her face and her huge dark eyes warmed.

"Gabriel. Congrats on an amazing match." She rose to her feet and flicked her hair over one shoulder. A hint of her rich, sexy scent wafted from the strands and he stiffened. Everywhere. Damn, she was dazzling.

"Merci." He reached for her small, strong hands and drew her in close. The callouses on her palms were rough and sensual against his skin. He brushed his lips on each cheek, in the traditional French greeting. She smelled delicious, like lavender and honey and her pale, creamy skin was silk beneath his lips. Time froze as he drank her in. They stood for a moment, impossibly close, their hands linked.

"Yes, great game." A male voice piped in.

Without releasing Dylan's hands, Gabriel turned to the short, stocky man who stood next to them. "Thank you. And you are?"

"Name's Cody. I'm a big fan. Great to meet you, Gabe. Welcome to California." The eager guy reached out a hand.

"Thank you. California is great. My name is Gabriel." No way in hell was anyone shortening his name. He kept one of Dylan's hands clasped in his, unwilling to break the connection, and shook Cody's with the other.

"The French don't use that kind of nickname." Dylan laughed and turned her gaze back to him and winked. "What are you drinking? Can I buy you some champagne?"

Drinks were free in the suite. But her flirtatious wink shot a spark of heat along his spine. "Absolutely."

He slid one arm around her waist and they sauntered to the bar together. The warmth from her skin seared along the side of his body. If he had his way, Dylan was coming home with him. Sooner than later.

His new teammates and a few familiar faces crowded around them. The Galaxy had given him a warm welcome and he'd effortlessly slipped into the rhythm of the established football club.

Today's victory confirmed he'd made the right move. Ever since he was a boy, he'd fantasized about moving to America with its promise of freedom, not to mention the distance from his responsibilities in France.

But his five-year contract lay ahead of him–days, weeks, and months to bond with his teammates and reach the pinnacle of his career. All the time in the world. Right now, with the high of scoring the winning goal behind him, he was ready to leave with Dylan.

Her melodic sweet voice, the gleam in her eyes, and the mischief in her smile were heating his blood. "Thanks for accepting my invitation. Will you join me for dinner so we can catch up?"

One dark brow arched and she paused with the champagne flute inches from her full, rosy lips. "Tonight? Don't you want to celebrate with your team?"

He held his breath, unfamiliar nerves kicking in. "Believe me, I'll be celebrating with them for the next five years. Right now, I'm more interested in reconnecting with you. So, oui, tonight."

She paused, her pink lips parted. "Well, I'd only planned on coming to the game."

He stroked a hand down her soft cheek. "But you ran away in the morning without saying goodbye. I'll forgive you if you come with me." He needed to spend time with her. To reconnect.

She froze at his touch, and a small line formed between her brows. "Ah, guilt. You're right, it was terribly rude of me to leave that way. But I don't want to get mobbed by the press and I'm afraid they'll be all over you."

"I already spoke to reporters down on the field, but you have a point." He set down the glass on the hard Formica bar top. "We can head back to my place to see the sunset on the ocean and order in." As an artist, wouldn't she enjoy the unobstructed ocean view?

"That could work. Where's your place?" She smiled.

Yes! Play it cool. "Not too far. Manhattan Beach."

Her full brows drew together over her small straight nose. "Ugh, traffic and parking is terrible there."

"Why don't I drive us and you can tell me what you've been doing since last summer. I'll bring you back to your car whenever you want."

"You just want to make sure I don't sneak out again, don't you?" Her lips twitched.

He laughed and triumph surged through him. "You've figured me out. Seriously though, traffic is awful."

Her lips curved up and she picked up her purse. "I'm all yours."

He sure as hell hoped so.

CHAPTER 2

GABRIEL DROVE THE WAY HE played soccer, and if memory served her, the way he made love. With intensity, power, and style. Dylan's pulse galloped and her skin tingled with awareness. Her memory hadn't failed her–his bronzed god profile made her fingers itch to draw him. Again. Not that she'd ever reveal those sketches she'd tucked away to anyone.

His strong, tanned hands lightly gripped the leather steering wheel of the sleek black BMW M6, easily maneuvering around other cars on the always-congested 405 Freeway. Each turn of the wheel highlighted the golden hair sprinkled on his lean muscular forearms. He'd been gorgeous in his apartment, but with the late afternoon Southern California light bathing him in a tawny glow, he was incredible. Her throat grew more parched each moment they got closer to his condo. She clasped her hands together and dug her nails into her palms. *Focus, girl.*

Maybe if they talked about mundane matters, the nerves skittering down her spine would settle. "So, did you buy a place or are you renting until you figure out where you want to be?"

Gabriel glanced over at her. "Renting with an option to buy. I'll see how much I like it this season. How far away do you live?"

"Hmmm…it's about an hour or two to Rancho Santa Fe, depending on the traffic. I don't come up here much, so not sure." No need to go into the myriad of reasons why she and her family avoided Los Angeles.

"What's it like there?"

"It's pretty much a private oasis away from the busy-ness of Southern California. My family owns a horse-breeding ranch and it's lush and green and lovely."

"You live with your family?" One dark brow arched over his sleek sunglasses.

Dylan nodded. "We've got tons of space. I basically have my own wing and my studio there."

"Sounds a little like my family's place in The Rhone Valley. Okay, here we are."

When she'd been chatting, he'd exited the freeway and curved down the well-groomed, charming tree-lined streets of Manhattan Beach. He pulled up in front of a sleek, modern white building on the corner of the boardwalk. A gleaming metallic garage door slid silently up and he navigated the sports car into the pristine space.

Before she could open the passenger door, he was there, extending his strong, square hand and assisting her out of the low-slung leather seat. Every single fiber of her being leapt to attention, from the top of her tingling scalp down to her toes. And everywhere in between. The palpable chemistry between them undulated, ebbing and flowing like the waves crashing on the beach nearby.

Hands linked, they ascended a single flight of broad wrought iron stairs. When he opened the large door, her lips parted in wonder at his home's simple classic beauty. Wide honey-colored plank flooring set off the soaring ceiling, stark white walls, and midnight navy couch and love-seat. Nothing distracted from the main attraction: enormous glass doors revealing the unobstructed view of the wide golden sand beach melting into the cobalt blue Pacific Ocean.

"Wow. So I guess you signed on the dotted line the minute you saw this view?" Dylan drank in the beauty of the late afternoon sky.

Gabriel's laugh was a low purr in his throat. "Exactly. Come." He slid the French doors open and led her out to an immense deck.

Immediately, the warm, salty breeze caressed her skin and the shriek of seagulls filled the early twilight sky. Streaks of mauve and raspberry and tangerine turned the horizon into a watercolor tableau worthy of its own canvas. She leaned against the white wooden railing and sighed with pleasure.

"This is amazing. When did you arrive and do you get to spend much time here?" The Major League Soccer season ran from March to December. Professional athletes didn't get much downtime, even in the off-season.

He was close enough that the clean fresh scent of soap and shampoo tickled her senses. His hair held a hint of curl and glints of chestnut and caramel. He angled his head toward her. "The transfer came through a few months ago, but I finished up my contract with Barcelona. I was at practice the morning after I arrived. So, no, I haven't spent enough time here yet."

"Thanks for sharing it with me."

He reached for her hand again, lacing their fingers together. "Let's have some wine and choose something to order for dinner. What are you in the mood for?"

"Italian or maybe French?" Her cheeks flamed. No innuendos there at all. Nope, not a one.

He waggled his eyebrows. "That can be arranged."

Before she could react, he pulled her into his arms and lowered his head. He paused a few inches from her lips and slid one hand up her back to clasp her head. His minty breath mingled with hers and her lips parted in anticipation. His pupils dilated, his eyes black. With a growl, he captured her mouth and stroked and swirled his tongue with hers.

She melted against him, her knees buckled, and only his powerful embrace saved her from sliding to the deck in a boneless heap. She wove her arms around him, gripping the thin material of his t-shirt.

"Get a room!" A shout from the boardwalk below doused them like a bucket of freezing water.

Gabriel's hold softened and Dylan stepped back.

She exhaled a shaky breath and smoothed back her hair. Worked to slow her thundering heartbeat and gather some composure. When she'd agreed to come over to his house, she'd been anticipating flirtation and conversation, but nothing could have prepared her for experiencing the intensity of their chemistry again. They'd only spent one night together, but he'd left an indelible impression on her. Apparently, it was mutual.

Gabriel flashed a cheeky grin. "I've got several rooms inside, care to join me?"

"Aren't you the clever one? Maybe we should slow things down and have that drink. And I am hungry." Everything about him was seductive and she was inexorably drawn to him. If she didn't at least gently tap the brakes, they'd be in bed before dinner. Or instead of dinner.

When he arched a brow and one side of his sculpted mouth twitched, she said, "For food."

"*Bien sur.* Of course. How do you feel about Chablis?" He gestured for her to precede him back into the condo.

"Chablis would be lovely." Dylan crossed the main floor to a large white granite island, which delineated the living space from the spacious modern kitchen.

"Please, have a seat." He gestured toward four indigo blue bar stools and sauntered with his customary catlike grace to two refrigerators on the far wall—one stainless steel and one glass-front, full of wine. He pulled out a bottle from a black wrought iron rack, grabbed two crystal glasses, and joined her.

The whisper of his French accent was almost as sexy as his long-fingered hands expertly uncorking the bottle of chilled white wine. Good lord, would she be able to resist him? Did she even want to?

He poured the pale golden liquid and handed her a glass. "Salut."

"Salut." She returned the traditional French toast and sipped the wine. "Mmm...that's delicious. What is it?"

He grimaced. "It's actually from my family's winery."

"DuVernay?" Heat rose in her cheeks. They'd shared DuVernay wine in bed last summer. Afterward, she'd learned his family owned one of the oldest vineyards in all of France.

He shrugged nonchalantly, his expression unreadable. "Oui."

"Do you spend much time there?" Was he as sensitive about his family's famous name as she was about her own?

"Not really. My father wants me to run the vineyards one day, but my sister is the one with the passion and skill. I'd prefer to settle here." He shrugged again before sitting next to her. "Tell me more about your art and where I can see it?" Gabriel's charming grin was back in place.

Settle, did he mean settle down? Her heartbeat accelerated. "Well, I focus primarily on landscapes and portraits, sort of a modern take on classical impressionism. I'm waiting to hear about a couple shows in Laguna Beach."

She'd been rejected by so many agents and galleries, staying optimistic she'd receive one "yes" was challenging.

"I'd love to see your paintings. I can tell you're talented." Interest gleamed in his feline green eyes.

"How can you tell?" She laughed. "Are you into art?"

"Yes, I'm into art. And I can tell from your passion. Your hands. You."

"Huh." Her palms prickled with moisture.

"Growing up, my sister and I spent a lot of time at museums and galleries. My mother wanted to paint, but didn't have the special gift, so now she is a connoisseur and collector."

"Oh." Dylan's gut clenched and she curled her fingers around the stem of her wineglass. Her greatest fear was her talent wasn't special enough to break out in the ridiculously competitive art world. Would she also end up a collector instead? It wasn't like she focused on cutting edge techniques or political messages, like some artists being noticed today. Nope, she just tried to capture the unique beauty of the moment, like many artists before her.

"Doesn't your father have connections? I mean, he's huge, non?" Gabriel's brows rose.

"I don't want to use the McNeill name. I want to get discovered in my own right." She shook her head. Had he followed her online over the last year too?

"I understand. Playing football was just for me. My family name didn't matter." He brushed two long fingers along her bare forearm and a shiver shimmered along her skin. "I would love to see your paintings."

"One day, if you're lucky." Flirting with Gabriel was as natural as breathing.

"I'm lucky because we're together again." He lifted her hand and kissed her palm.

Dylan melted at his easy charm. "You're smooth. But will I have to hide from your fan club and all the photographers chasing you?"

He shook his head. "No. It should not be so over the top here. No complications. And you are who I wanted to see once I learned I'd be in California."

Her belly tightened. "I'm not sure I'd call you uncomplicated, but I'm glad you called me." He was a walking complication, but completely irresistible.

He pressed a soft kiss against her lips and hopped up. "Let me grab the iPad."

When he headed out of the room, she tucked the loose strand of hair teasing her cheek behind her ear and blew out a shaky breath. Last time when they'd hooked up, she'd been in a reckless mood and seeking an escape. One-night stands were not her usual style.

Then again, they'd already been together one night, so wasn't this just a continuation? Today's reunion was much more complex than she'd expected. Of course, she'd figured they might end up sleeping together again, but hadn't contemplated more, not when he was embarking on the most important stage of his career and she was determined to pursue her dreams.

No more commissioned horse paintings—no, she wanted recognition for creations born from her own inspiration. Major recognition. Although she and her sisters shunned any type of media attention and didn't want their names associated with fame, fortune, or scandal ever again. A clear wall existed between the type of attention given to artists and to actors–new paintings didn't generate tabloid interest.

When Gabriel returned from his study, he smiled at the picture Dylan made seated at his kitchen island, resting her chin on her hand, watching the waning sunlight. Damn, she was breathtaking. Their night last year had been more than a casual lay–and the more he learned about her, the more fascinated he became.

Thank god he'd followed his gut instinct to reach out to her. He didn't have some elaborate plan, but now they were living in the same state, he wanted to explore the strongest connection he'd ever experienced.

Tonight, they'd enjoy the sunset together and share a delicious meal. Perhaps enjoy each other. Maybe after dinner he could convince her to allow him to take her back to her car in the morning.

"Now that's a wicked grin if I've ever seen one."
Dylan's lips quirked at the corners.

He laughed. "Me? Wicked? I'm just excited to
share dinner with you, that's all." His hands itched
to grab her hair and pull her back against him.
Hard. But now wasn't the time. Patience wasn't
one of his big virtues, but he'd give it a shot.

One dark elegant brow arched. "Of course, I'm
sure that's all you're excited about."

His pulse quickened at her snappy banter and
breezy confidence. He crossed the last few steps to
where she perched on the barstool. "Who is the
wicked one?"

"I don't know what you mean. I'm starving.
Let's order dinner." Her enormous doe eyes were
heavy-lidded and her pink tongue darted out to
lick her lips.

He stiffened. *Damn.* "Definitely." He snatched
up the tablet.

"This one has incredible seafood and pasta,
of course. What do you think?" He turned the
screen so she could see the local Italian restaurant
he'd selected and her pink lips curved up.

She clapped her hands together. "Yum. Shrimp
scampi please. With linguine."

"I was going to order that. Should I order the
halibut instead and we can share?"

"Oh, I'm not going to share. You should probably order your own." She shook her head.

"No sharing?" He laughed at her enthusiasm.

"I'm selfish like that. I'll offer you a taste, but
no more." She grinned.

"Greedy. I like it. I will claim my taste now." He leaned in and nibbled on her soft lips.

Her quick gasp and instant response revealed she wasn't immune. Not even close. Her breath was sweet, with hints of the wine still on her tongue, and some flavor unique to her. The scent from her hair and the warmth of her silky skin next to him tested his self-control. Every muscle hardened and before he lost control, he stepped back and grinned down at her.

Her lips twitched. "I don't know if I'm greedy, but my twin sister eats like a Viking and growing up I had to guard my food or she'd polish off my plate before I had a chance."

He laughed. "I promise I'll keep my hands to myself. At least with your meal."

She flicked her gaze down toward her hands, her expressive eyes hidden from him. A rosy flush appeared on her chest and traveled up the creamy skin on her slender neck and stained her high cheekbones. Damn, Mademoiselle Dylan Marie McNeill intrigued him with her mix of laughter and seduction. He couldn't wait to learn everything about her.

For now, she was with him, lived in the same state, and he wouldn't be flying off to another country anytime soon. No, he was in the land of freedom for good.

When his agent shared the outrageous sum the Galaxy was willing to pay for him, he'd jumped at the offer. His father had been furious, of course, but part of their deal was that he would finish out his soccer career before acquiescing to family obligations. Being the eldest son came with archaic duties—ones he didn't care to shoulder. His father acted like they lived in 1895 instead of the 21st century. He wasn't the son of a damn duke.

Now he'd help his younger sister Claude fulfill her dreams and prove to their father she should run the DuVernay vineyards. Then he'd be able to create a life he wanted, not be forced into a pre-ordained one.

"Voila. Dinner will be here in thirty minutes. I love this service you have here." Not that Barcelona didn't have delicious seafood, but not delivered with a few keystrokes.

"No Door Dash in Europe?" Dylan sipped her wine.

Her luscious mouth distracted him again. *Focus.* "Not really. Barcelona was starting one, but not in Paris that I've seen."

"Makes sense. So you have places in Barcelona and Paris? And here?" She tilted her head to the side, her auburn hair shimmering against her skin.

"Yes. And my family home is in Sablet, a small town in Provence. Let's go outside, oui?" He picked up their wine and followed her onto the deck. He forced himself to admire the sunset instead of focusing solely on her cute butt in her snug white jeans.

She angled her head back toward him. "The sky looks almost bruised with the deep purples and blues. You're really lucky with this incredible view."

He slid his arm around her and gazed into her eyes. "Yes, I am."

She laughed and stepped back, creating some space between them. Too much space. "Don't give me all your cheesy soccer-lebrity lines. I'm here. You don't need to."

"Hey." He pressed one hand against his heart. "Me, cheesy?"

She chuckled. "You know women don't stand a chance against your French charm."

"You hurt me, Dylan. Of course I mean it—you really are more breathtaking than any sunset." And he did mean it.

"Sure." She laughed again, smoothing her long mane over one shoulder.

He reached for her hand. "It's not a line. Don't make assumptions about me, okay?" Suddenly it was important she realize he was genuine.

Her gaze was searching. "Okay. But don't feel like you need to flatter me. And I know that most celebrity stories aren't true. I learned that lesson long ago."

His chest tightened at the hint of seriousness in her warm chocolate eyes. He caught himself before he made another glib reply, his default. "I'd like to know you better."

Her rosy lips curved up. "I'd like to know you better too."

They stared at each other for a moment and for the second time in one day, Gabriel hesitated. Uncertain of his next move. The buzz of conversations on the beach below and the brush of salty air on his cheeks filled the air.

The doorbell rang, breaking the moment. Their gazes remained locked for another second and then once again she swept hers away and turned toward the living room.

"Scampi time." She grinned and sauntered across the deck inside.

While he refilled their wineglasses, Dylan arranged the two Scampi linguine on his Provence-style canary yellow and peacock blue patterned plates.

"Thanks for dinner." She clinked her glass against his and dove into her Scampi.

He tried not to stare as her small even white teeth sank into the large shrimp. He tried not to moan when she hummed low in her throat after she swallowed her first bite. *Mon Dieu*, no way in hell would he make it through dinner if she was going to eat like that. He loved seeing a woman enjoy her food, but all he could picture was her sinking her teeth into him...anywhere she wanted. He quickly averted his eyes and focused on his own plate.

"*C'est délicieux*." And that's all he had. Elle est vraiment délicieuse. He hadn't forgotten how she tasted.

They ate for a few minutes in companionable silence.

"This is incredible. Oh my god. If I lived up here I'd eat this every night." She sighed and set down her fork. "Don't you have to watch what you eat for your career?"

"Yes and no. It's more about being strong and being as fast as I can. If I'm too heavy, I can't run. But I eat well, just like I did at home." In France, food was all about pleasure.

She nodded. "That makes sense. And the wine?" She waved her glass.

"Some guys don't drink during the season or the night before a match. I grew up in the vineyards. My parents gave me wine mixed with water when I was six years old. It's just, you know, enjoyment?"

"Yes, enjoyment. Today has definitely been enjoyable. Would you be disappointed if I asked you to take me back to my car soon? I've got a big day tomorrow." She smiled, softening the blow of her words.

Zut. "On one condition." He shifted off the bar stool and drew her down into his arms, savoring the slide of every inch of her against him.

She slid her slender arms around his waist. "Yes?" She whispered.

"Promise me I'll see you again this week." He tilted her chin up and gazed into her dark eyes. His heart was racing, like he'd just sprinted down the field.

She nodded and he lowered his mouth and murmured against her sweet lips. "I'll be counting the hours, beautiful."

And taking freezing showers until he could hold her again.

CHAPTER 3

ADRENALINE COURSED THROUGH GABRIEL'S VEINS and the sweet taste of impending victory filled him. The sweet Southern California sunshine, pristine blue sky, and mild summer breeze set the perfect backdrop for another Galaxy win. Toronto FC's team was going down.

Munoz and he passed and flicked the ball like they had all the time in the world, navigating down the field with control and style. With only a few minutes remaining in the second half, Gabriel prepared to score the winning goal. Mind crystal clear and focus unfettered, he advanced toward the goal line.

Damn he loved this game.

"We love you, Gabriel!" A loud cheer rose from the stands, pulling him out of the moment and he glanced up for a split second.

A split second too long.

Excruciating pain blasted through him and he plunged down onto the grass. Suddenly, everything shifted into slow motion, like when a serial killer stalks you in a nightmare, but you're trapped in quicksand. A snapping sound, like the crunching of autumn branches beneath your feet exploded in his ears. Pressure from the sharp elbow of the opposing team's defender as he shoved into him and hooked one ankle around his. One of the oldest dirty tricks in the game.

A red card offense if anyone caught it.

His knee shattered as it twisted in an angle it was never meant to achieve. The earth beneath him was unforgiving–like slamming into concrete.

Gritting his teeth, he shifted up onto his elbow, and then crumpled back to the grass. *Mon Dieu.* He blinked against the glare of the now unfriendly California sunshine. An eerie silence reigned in the stadium. Harsh pants filled the air–his own ragged breath. A feathery cloud shaped like a hawk offered a hint of relief by floating across the bright blue sky. Numbness bathed through him and he allowed his lids to close.

Normally, he'd pop up off the ground. He'd fallen a million times since he first kicked a soccer ball as a toddler. Getting up immediately was key. Get up. Keep going. Play through the pain. Sink into an ice bath later. Let the team doc tape you up or the physical therapist massage away the knots. Never be distracted until the winning goal was scored.

The game always came first. Always.

When hands reached for him and voices surrounded him, his eyes flew open.

"Stay still, we've got you." Dr. Reynolds, the

team doctor, peered down at him.

"Keep breathing, Gabe." Some random person butchered his name, but he didn't have the strength to correct him. Why did these damn people insist on shortening Gabriel?

"We're going to turn you over onto your back now. Try not to help us."

He snorted through the pain. Like he could move his damn leg. Right now it felt like he'd been caught in some barbaric torture device, like the knee crusher he'd seen on a trip to some medieval museum in a Tuscan hill town last year.

He struggled to steady his breathing. His heartbeat thundered in his temples and ice shrouded his skin, despite the warm afternoon. His fingers curled into fists.

"Can you relax your hands please, Gabriel? I need to take your blood pressure." The soothing tones of Cathleen, one of the trainers and a physician's assistant, murmured. He forced his hands to unclench.

Then, he was lifted onto a stretcher and placed on one of the golf cart pallets. He winced as ice was packed around his left leg and everything jostled, despite the four guys lifting him like he was one of his maman's delicate china espresso cups. *Merde*.

Applause filled the stadium and he raised one arm and waved at the crowd when they rolled him off the field. No reason to alert the fans of the undeniable truth: his career was finished.

Back in the stadium's medical facility, voices

buzzed around him.

"We need to get him to the hospital ASAP, I need to operate today. His knee is destroyed." Dr. Reynolds, Orthopedic surgeon to the L.A. Galaxy and the L.A. Chargers was considered one of the best sports medicine surgeons in the country.

For some reason, Gabriel's hearing was sharp as a bat's right now. Murmurs from a few people he didn't recognize off in the corner floated to his ears.

"Damn, this is tragic. I mean, he just started his contract here and all that money—"

"Shut up, Bill. He might hear you and that won't help."

"Well, I mean, come on, they paid a small fortune and he gets injured almost right away." The guy whispered, but not quietly enough.

"Like it was his fault they play dirty. Just shut up or get out of here." His defender snapped.

Silence.

"Gabriel, I'm going to tell you what's going on and what we need to do, okay?"

Dr. Reynolds's round, kind face smiled down at him.

He gritted his teeth—hell, had he stopped gritting his teeth—and gave a curt nod.

"I'm going to tell it to you straight. From my physical exam, it looks like your patella may be shattered. Your meniscus and other ligaments are also likely damaged or torn. We need to get you to the hospital and do quick x-rays and an MRI. We need to move fast."

Gabriel bit his lip, enjoying the shift of pain there. "Will I play again?" He knew the answer. Knew it in his heart and his soul. His life was over.

Dr. Reynolds' expression didn't alter, not even a flicker of his eyes. Great poker face. "I can't make predictions. Let's see what's going on in there and go from there. Okay?"

Gabriel's eyes squeezed shut, welcoming the blackness. What the hell had he expected? What did it matter now? Unless they could give him a bionic knee, he'd never regain his speed or agility. He was old–thirty-one–not some teenager who might be able to overcome it.

"Gabriel?" Cathleen asked.

He nodded curtly. "Yeah."

"The ambulance is waiting. I'll ride with you. Is there anyone you want me to call?" Her firm voice was soothing.

"Non. Let's go." Dylan's face popped into his mind, but he wouldn't burden her.

Dylan cursed under her breath and tossed her paintbrush on the stool where her supplies sat. Her stupid phone had been droning incessantly in the pocket of her loose, flowered sundress. Interruptions could yank her out of her creative zone and cost her hours trying to regain focus.

Usually, she avoided keeping the distracting device with her when she was working, but she was waiting to hear from Gabriel a little later, finalizing the details of their date tonight. The last week had been full of flirtatious texts and late night phone calls, each one more intimate than the next. Although she'd hoped to see him sooner, their schedules hadn't meshed. But she'd already packed an overnight bag, complete with new lingerie and an outfit for the morning.

Unlike her premature exit in Paris, this time she'd promised to stay for croissants and café au lait.

She tapped on the screen and saw a missed call and several text alerts from her best friend, Lily, in France. Her scalp prickled and the fine hairs on the nape of her neck stood up. Her best friend could keep a secret and she'd confided in Lily about seeing Gabriel again.

Each message demanded whether she'd seen the news about Gabriel. Nothing from Gabriel himself, but he'd been playing. Her fingers trembled as she opened her browser and typed in his name. Immediately, headlines flashed up with photos of him being carried off the field on a stretcher. *Soccer Star's Career Finished? LA Galaxy's Million Dollar Man Done Already? Dirty Play a Career Ender for DuVernay?*

Dylan's eyes filled as she skimmed the highlights where terms like "shattered knee" and "career ending" jumped out.

She texted Gabriel, but didn't anticipate a response. By now, he was probably at the hospital or even already in surgery. She tapped out a short reply to Lily and rushed out of the studio. No time to clean up her paints. Gabriel needed her now—she could feel it in her gut. In her heart.

She sprinted down the hallway and practically plowed through her older sister.

"Hey, slow down. What's going on?" Amanda clasped her shoulders, her clear green eyes narrowed in concern.

Dylan's breath whooshed out. "Can I fill you in later? I need to change and get up to L.A." She hurried down the wide hallway toward her bedroom. She didn't have time for a long discussion, not when Gabriel's life could be imploding.

Amanda fell into step beside her. "Slow down and tell me. Who is in L.A.? You can't drive like this, I'm afraid you'll have an accident."

Damn, her sister was always so protective. "Okay, remember the hot French soccer player from last summer? Well, he's in L.A. now, playing for the Galaxy. I saw him last weekend and was supposed to see him tonight. He got injured today and is in the hospital." Urgency pounded through her and her pulse was thrumming.

"Oh no, that's terrible. Did he ask you to come?" Amanda's voice deepened with concern.

Dylan shook her head and pulled her old paint-splattered sundress over her head and strode into her ensuite bathroom. "No, Lily saw it on the news and told me. They're saying his career might be over."

She flicked on the shower and wound her hair up into a knot on top of her head. No time for anything more than a quick rinse—it wasn't like she'd be wearing that silky lingerie tonight.

"Dylan, hold on a minute. You're rushing to his bedside after he had a major injury? What if..." Her sister's brow furrowed.

Dylan stepped into the shower. "What if what? We had plans tonight. He's alone and his family is in France. I can't let him wake up from surgery by himself."

"Whoa, Dylan. I thought you hooked up with him in Paris and now you're saying you saw him again here and you're running up there? Why don't you wait until you hear from him first–he might not feel like seeing anyone if the damage is as serious as you say." Amanda frowned.

Dylan flicked off the water and stepped out onto the fluffy bathmat. Amanda handed her a towel and she dried herself as she entered her huge walk-in closet. Rows of floaty dresses blurred her vision and she randomly snatched a kelly green sleeveless one and yanked it over her head. She stuffed her feet into some golden gladiator flat sandals.

"Hello? Are you listening to me?" Her sister hovered.

She fought to keep the exasperation out of her voice. "Yes. I hear you. My gut is telling me to go and I'm going. Okay?" She turned to her beloved older sister, who had been more like a mom to her after their mom died.

Amanda sighed. "I know you think I'm too cautious and you know I think you're too impulsive. Just promise me you'll be careful and don't freak out if he isn't happy to see you. I just know how sensitive you are and don't want to see you hurt."

Dylan wrapped her arms around her sweet sister. "I love you. If he doesn't want me to be there, I'll know that I tried, okay? I need to go. And I promise not to drive too fast." She crossed her fingers behind her sister's back on that teensy white lie.

Amanda squeezed her tight and Dylan savored the warmth and strength her sister exuded for a few precious seconds. She wanted to offer that same warmth and strength to Gabriel when he woke up. Although they were newly involved, she'd reminisced about him for over a year and her intuition never failed her. He needed her.

Now if she could find out where they'd taken him by the time she arrived in L.A…

CHAPTER 4

GABRIEL'S FINGERS CURLED INTO FISTS and he battled the hopelessness filling him. Despite trying to use his meditation techniques to remain calm, he was spiraling into a pit of fury and despair. He glared at the tubes in his arms and beeping monitors and fought the urge to rip off the tape and pull out the tubes and…grab a wheelchair?

It wasn't like he could make a dramatic exit and run out.

If he could ever run again.

He sagged deeper into the crisp hospital sheets and exhaled. The pain was unspeakable and they'd avoided giving him too much medication because surgery was imminent. He'd been at the Harbor UCLA Medical Center forever. Why didn't they just get the damned operation over with—what did it matter now?

A young nurse came to check his vitals again and handed Gabriel his phone. Apparently Cathleen, his favorite trainer, had brought his things from his locker, including his street clothes and phone. Not that he wanted to deal with anybody.

But looking at his phone had to be better than staring at the machines monitoring him.

He frowned at the screen. One hundred and twenty texts? Fifty voicemails? Seriously? Damn reporters. His eyes widened when Dylan's name popped up. They'd had a date planned tonight– one more thing ruined.

Gabriel, I'm on my way up there. Please tell me which hospital you're in.

His chest tightened. She was on the way? Warmth filled him.

Harbor-UCLA. Probably heading into surgery soon. I'll give your name to the staff so they'll let you in. The nurses had informed him the press was downstairs, so security was tight and nobody could come up to his room without clearance. It wasn't like the Galaxy wanted speculation about their most expensive acquisition.

Be there soon.

Although the situation was a disaster, relief filled him knowing she cared enough to come up.

Another message popped up, this time from his sister, Claude. *Zut.* Although this nightmare had commenced a few short hours ago, his family already knew. Claude never missed one of his matches, but did his parents know too?

Because all the meditation in the world wouldn't be able to protect him from his father's reaction. His father would be waltzing on one of his priceless antique tables in the family chateau. If Gabriel's soccer career were over, he'd have no choice but to return and assume the mantle of head of DuVernay Vineyards. At least in his father's mind there would be no question.

Gabriel wasn't much for prayer, despite being raised Catholic. But now he prayed to whatever higher power might help him keep his career, stay in the U.S., and convince his father that his sister was the natural person to assume control of the family business. He'd figured he had five years to devise a plan.

Five years for his father to pull his head out of his ass and see what was right in front of him: Claude was the natural successor and Gabriel was not. Sure, for the last two hundred years or so, the DuVernay custom dictated the heir to running the winery be the oldest son. Gabriel's father had followed in the footsteps of his grand-père, great grand-père, and great-great grand-père without question. Tradition was not to be denied according to Didier DuVernay.

Despite Gabriel, Claude, and their mother attempting to convince his dad times had changed and the winery should go to Claude, his father had dug in his heels. No amount of reason or shouting matches budged the man a millimeter.

If Gabriel had to figure it out now, he had no frickin' clue how. All he'd been focused upon was winning. The only mantle he wanted to assume was that of best soccer player in history. He needed more time to help raise his beloved sport's prominence in North America.

He needed these next five years.

He couldn't be finished. Not yet. Not now. Not

like this.

His life was over.

"Mr. DuVernay?" A timid voice pulled him from his brooding.

He opened his eyes and stared at the round-faced nurse before him. "Yes?"

"Dr. Reynolds wants to get you down to pre-op now. He said he'll explain everything to you about the procedure before he begins."

Gabriel bit the inside of his lip. "Do I have a choice?"

She raised one hand up to her cheek. "A choice, I don't think—"

"It's okay. I'm ready. But, I have a friend coming to see me. Can you make sure she's allowed up?"

She nodded. "Of course, of course. Let me write down her name."

She scribbled down Dylan's name onto the paper stacked on the clipboard in her hands.

An orderly entered the room with a gurney and the nurse held out her hand and took his phone. "The doctor will explain everything. I'll put your phone with your things. It's all going to be fine." She smiled at him, but her eyes reflected concern.

Gabriel dropped his head back on the starched pillow and closed his eyes. Maybe there would be a miracle.

Dylan ascended from the bowels of the hospital's mammoth parking garage. Just how many people were being treated in the place? She'd had to keep winding down into what felt like the center of the earth to find a parking space.

On the drive from Rancho Santa Fe, she'd alternated between wondering if she'd been rash zooming up here or if she should have waited until after he'd had surgery. All she knew was her gut screamed that he was alone and needed a friend. Her heart ached imagining how he must be feeling right now—alone in a new country, seriously injured, and fearful of having his dreams snatched away. If she could comfort him, driving up to the hospital wouldn't be a mistake. She wasn't acting like a lovesick teenager—they'd had plans tonight after all.

Her calves protested as she continued climbing the stairs, all twelve flights of them. She needed the physical exertion to soothe her nerves prior to seeing him in person. Because she wasn't sure what his condition would be, she wanted to be reassuring. Hopefully, his leg looked better than what the sensationalistic news reports were proclaiming.

By the time she finally reached the lobby, the tissue-thin material of her striped green sundress was glued to her shoulder blades. The darned garage was probably over one hundred degrees and the stairs had been steep. She wiped away the dampness on the back of her neck—thank goodness she'd piled her hair into a topknot.

She opened the door into the main lobby and the noise slammed into her like a wall. She staggered back a few steps and gazed around the crowded area. Super high ceilings and huge windows should have given the room an open, light feeling, but the cacophony and crowds of people made it feel more like the mosh pit at a death metal concert. Back in high school, some boy took her to one of those concerts. She'd despised it then, and hated it even more now.

Forcing herself to breath slowly in and out of her nose, she gripped her purse and began making her way to what appeared to be the main check in area. *Inhale for four. Exhale for four. Repeat.* She'd only made it a few steps when someone shoved against her shoulder. Hard.

"Hey, watch out. Some of us are here because it's a hospital. Have a little respect." She pushed back against the tall, hulking guy with slicked back dark hair. He had a camera around his neck and video equipment under his arm.

"Chill out Red. We've got the right to be here. The soccer dude is big news. Have you heard of the First Amendment?"

Dylan narrowed her eyes. Rude jerk. Red? "I need to actually see a patient, so move."

He rolled his eyes and turned his back. Dylan pushed past him and ducked under his long arm. She wasn't going to put up with this crap, especially not from leech paparazzi hoping to profit off of someone's misfortune. Outrage fueled her steps.

She gritted her teeth and continued to push through the tightly knit crowd. Perspiration slicked her skin and her pulse hammered in her temples.

An elbow slammed into her back and propelled her forward. If the information desk hadn't been right there, she would have sprawled out onto her face on the hard tile floors. Clinging to the solid edge, she managed to steady herself. Memories from thirteen years ago flashed through her mind. Paparazzi had pursued her down one of her high school's hallways–she'd tripped and landed on all fours. She still had the scars on her knees to prove it.

The incident was the final straw that convinced her father to chuck his career as the top director/producer in Hollywood and move their family down to Pacific Vista Ranch to start a new life. A private, secluded life until last summer, when the paparazzi had discovered them and raked the story of her mom's tragic death through the coals again.

Her belly twisted into knots and a headache started as a clamp on the back of her skull. *Oh no.* This media mob was here for Gabriel. If she got involved with him, she and her family would be subjected to all of this unwanted attention too. *Crap.* No way could she handle this on a regular basis.

She squared her shoulders–he was here now and she'd battled her way up to the information desk. She wasn't leaving until she saw Gabriel. Plenty of time to worry about the rest later.

She leaned in toward the harried looking middle-aged woman behind the counter and whispered, "Hi there, I'm on a list to go up to the orthopedic wing. Can I just show you my ID and text the name of the person so this mob doesn't hear?" She handed her the phone.

"Well security is coming to move them all out-side and not a moment too soon." The woman checked Dylan's screen and glanced up, eyes wide with speculation.

Dylan's heart and her head were pounding now. She needed to get out of this crowded lobby pronto or she was going to scream.

"Okay, Ms. McNeill, please go see the security guard at the east bank of elevators down the hall-way. Please keep your ID out to show him." She returned Dylan driver's license.

Before she could move, a wave of fresh air poured in, cooling the back of her neck.

"Everyone not visiting a patient outside. Now." The LAPD had arrived. Wow, Harbor-UCLA Medical Center wasn't messing around.

Protests echoed off the high ceilings, but the surge of lemmings reversed direction, leaving her with some personal space and an open path to the elevators. Thank god.

Dylan squared her shoulders, softened her death grip on the leather strap of her satchel-purse, and pivoted toward the elevators. She crossed the enormous lobby without incident and handed her ID to the brawny uniformed guard with a silver buzz cut who was guarding the elevator entrances. He studied her ID and crosschecked it with an iPad. After what felt like an hour, he returned her driver's license, unhooked the barrier rope, and gestured for her to pass.

"Elevator 4. It's pre-programmed to the patient's floor. Check in with the desk right after you get off and they'll provide you with further instructions," he said in a deep monotone.

The metallic doors swooshed open silently and Dylan entered the shiny box. The doors closed behind her and she flashed back to the days of attending her parents' movie premieres or other events. Discretion and privacy had been top priorities. Before everything fell apart, she and her sisters had found it exciting. Not so much anymore.

Why hadn't she considered how famous Gabriel was? When she'd been in Europe, it was standard to see him in a pair of boxer briefs showing off his eight-pack on the side of a bus or billboard. Although he wasn't as big a star in America, constant displays of his singular talent popped up regularly online. Not that she'd been searching his name or anything.

And nobody could have missed the screaming headlines proclaiming his astronomical deal with the L.A. Galaxy.

Again, she simply hadn't thought any of this through. No, over the last week, she'd been falling for him more with every text and phone call. Doodling his name on her sketchpad and daydreaming about seeing him again. Deep in her heart, she'd conceded her feelings were more than fleeting and wondered if his move to California was fate giving them another chance.

Until she'd experienced the mob downstairs waiting for news on Gabriel's injury, she hadn't been overly concerned. Nobody had noticed them leaving his match last weekend–only a week ago–and Gabriel had made it clear he welcomed a lower-profile life in California.

Being involved with Gabriel would throw a wrench into living a private life. Artists didn't garner the same type of attention and she'd sworn never to live in the public eye again. She pressed a hand to her aching stomach, disappointment flooding her veins.

No way would she risk attracting attention as Gabriel's latest fling. Although she'd planned on spending the night with him tonight–they'd already slept together, after all–it was probably for the best.

She'd show up for him here. Be a friend. But it could never go beyond that.

The doors opened, revealing the nurse's station in front of her. She swallowed the bitter taste lingering in her throat, squared her shoulders, and marched down the corridor.

CHAPTER 5

DYLAN SHIFTED AGAIN ON THE rigid, incredibly uncomfortable plastic seat in the hospital waiting area. She checked her watch and grimaced. She'd been at the hospital for three hours with no updates on Gabriel's condition. A glance out of the sole window in the cramped space confirmed neither the news vans nor the throngs of reporters had abandoned their vigils. Like Gabriel would walk out the front door of the hospital and give a press conference. Yeah right.

The room was empty except for a lean, medium-height blond man who had been pacing around the room for the last few hours, never able to sit for more than a few minutes at a time. They hadn't spoken. Was he here for Gabriel too or some other VIP patient?

An enormous bald man in a white coat approached. "Coach Davis and Ms. McNeill?"

"I'm Dr. Walsinky. Come with me to Mr. DuVernay's room where I can update you. He should be out of recovery in the next hour or so. He's waking from the anesthesia."

Dylan and Coach Davis followed the surgeon

down the hallway. She studied the man beside her—no wonder he seemed so miserable if he was Gabriel's coach. When they entered a massive corner suite, Dylan gasped.

Hospital room wasn't an accurate description of what looked more like a penthouse in a Five Star hotel. An enormous bed was set up close to the floor-to-ceiling windows. Luxurious silver drapes shrouded the golden California sun and created a shaded, protective atmosphere. Another symbol of Gabriel's considerable fortune and special treatment. Not that all the money in the world could give him back his health or career.

The doctor gestured for them to sit on a cushy beige couch. He cleared his throat. "I'll fill you in on what you need to know so you can be prepared when Mr. DuVernay returns. He will be awake, but he's got morphine in his system, so he could be a little disoriented."

"Wait a second." Coach Davis turned to Dylan. "You've signed an NDA, right?"

She stiffened. Before she could reply, Dr. Walsinky answered. "Mr. DuVernay requested Ms. McNeill be here."

Davis held up a hand. "That's fine. Sorry. It's just been a rough day."

The doctor gazed between them, with a faint frown. "I'll continue."

Dylan clasped her hands in her lap and squeezed tight. Now her decision to speed up to the hospital seemed precipitous. Especially after seeing the paparazzi and realizing his fame was a huge deterrent to them really having any type of relationship. Today could possibly be the last time she saw him.

The doctor's deep voice pulled her from her ruminations. "His patella has been shattered and basically every ligament and tendon is torn. He'll have to have another surgery. Most likely, he's going to either have to have plates put in or even have the knee replaced."

"Replaced? Shattered?" Gabriel's coach groaned and dropped his head into his hands.

"Are you sure?" Dylan whispered and bit her lip. Tears welled in her eyes and she struggled to gather her composure. No surgery existed that could fix him so he could run and perform like the top player in the world.

Dr. Walsinky peered down his imperious nose at her. "The damage is extensive. As I said, I've cleaned it up for now. We're consulting with a few other surgeons and he'll have the best care and options available."

"But it doesn't look good." Davis looked up, revealing his bleak expression.

The doctor shook his head. "Look, he'll walk, and possibly without a limp. But his career? If he were eighteen or even twenty years old and had a few years to rehab, but at his age…"

"That's terrible." Dylan looked down at her hands and her heart cracked for Gabriel. How was she going to be able to act hopeful and happy with him? She wasn't an actress like her mom had been. To say she wore her emotions on her sleeve was being generous in the best of times. *Crap.*

"Well, this information is to prepare you. Please don't share anything with him until I and the other doctors have briefed him."

"Of course." Dylan nodded, fighting back tears.

"Right." Davis nodded, but looked like he might cry too.

After a moment, the doctor spoke. "Why don't you both return to the waiting room and let the staff settle Mr. DuVernay in without an audience. Someone will let you know when he's ready for visitors." The doctor turned his attention back to the aluminum clipboard in his hands.

Dylan trailed behind Davis into the deserted hallway. At least the rabid press hadn't invaded.

"I'm going down to the cafeteria. I've got some calls to make." Coach Davis hurried away down the hall.

Dylan remained rooted to the spot. She didn't want to brave the cafeteria in case the media had infiltrated somehow and with her nerves quaking, caffeine was the last thing she needed. She leaned against the pale green wall, inhaled a cleansing breath, and released it slowly. Her heart raced in her chest.

"*Bonjour, mon chérie.*" A husky voice said.

Dylan looked up to see Gabriel on a gurney, his head propped up on a pillow, and a blindingly white sheet tucked up under his square jaw. Two staff in powder blue scrubs wheeled him into the room.

"You're awake." Her stomach clenched–he'd

called her his sweetheart.

One corner of his sculpted mouth quirked up. "Something like that. You coming in?" His voice was raspier than usual.

Somehow even sexier, despite the circumstances.

"Do you need a moment to get settled? I can wait." She didn't want him to feel obliged to invite her in, especially when they moved him to his bed. It all seemed incredibly intimate.

He shook his head. "Non, that's okay. Please."

She followed them into the room and headed straight to the large windows. While the attendants helped Gabriel into the bed, she studied the sun disappearing from the darkening afternoon sky. Had it only been a week ago they'd admired the vibrant streaks of color in the twilight horizon from his balcony?

"You can turn around now. I'm decent." His voice held a hint of humor.

How could he be resilient enough to joke around right now?

She turned and approached his bedside and deepened her grip on her purse. When she got emotional, she tended to talk with her hands, so it was safer to curb the tendency if she had any hope of appearing controlled and comforting.

No crying. No clues.

Just compassion and support.

"So," he murmured.

"So. How do you feel now?" She focused on his lean handsome face.

"Well, they pumped me full of some drugs, so I actually feel kind of like I drank a bottle of champagne. Or Irish whisky. You look enchantée."

Dylan's eyes widened because his French accent was dominating his flawless English. Even post-surgery, his voice mesmerized her. "Umm, merci."

"Good news is I can't feel my knee right now. It hurt like nothing I've ever experienced. I hope they were able to fix it and I'll be good as new." Gabriel's eyelids lowered to half-mast, his words slurred, and his head lolled forward.

She tentatively brushed his arm and his eyes opened. "Gabriel, I'm glad you aren't in pain now. Did they tell you how long you'd be here? Anything?"

"No, nothing." His eyelids flickered shut again. "Merci for coming. I think I'll be sleeping a while. Will you come back tomorrow? Please?"

Dylan's heart contracted. She leaned down and pressed a soft kiss on his lean cheek. As she stepped back, his bright green eyes flew open, pinning her with his gaze.

"Promise?" He murmured.

"Of course." The raw pain in his beautiful eyes jolted her. How could she refuse?

"Au demain. Tomorrow."

Dylan watched the grooves around his firm mouth soften as he drifted to sleep. She'd return to see him one more time.

One final time.

CHAPTER 6

WHISPERING VOICES INTRUDED INTO GABRIEL'S pleasant cocoon. He and Dylan were floating on their backs, holding hands in the balmy Mediterranean Sea, right off the coast of the island of Corsica. Rays of golden sunshine warmed his face and satisfaction filled him–life with the beautiful redhead couldn't be more perfect.

Something brushed across his cheek and he frowned. What kind of bug would interrupt his idyllic afternoon? He'd just swat it away.

"Gabriel. *Tu te réveilles.* Wake up."

He resisted opening his eyelids, which were heavy sandbags aiding him in his quest to remain in heaven. Was that really his father's voice? How had his perfect dream morphed into a nightmare?

"*Mon frère.* My brother." Claude too? What was going on?

Finally, her urgent tone penetrated the surface and with a herculean effort, he pried his eyes open. His father, mother, and sister hovered over him. He closed his eyes and scrubbed his hands across his face before glancing up again.

"How are you here? What time is it?" It all came rushing back. The accident. The operation. *Merde*. He scowled and looked toward the windows, but heavy silver draperies obscured the sky.

His beloved younger sister leaned against the bedrails and her moss green eyes, so like his own, shone with unshed tears. "It's noon on Monday. We saw the match and booked the company jet right away. Gabriel, I'm so sorry."

"*Mon fils, je suis désolée.* How do you feel?" His maman stepped up beside his sister and reached for his hand. Her delicate eyebrows knit together in concern. His father merely stood silently, his lean hawk-like face stern.

Before he could respond, a petite middle-aged woman with curly silver hair appeared. "You're awake, Mr. DuVernay. Are you ready for some breakfast?"

"I'd like to speak with the doctor." Screw breakfast. He wanted answers. Now.

The woman smiled gently. "Let me bring you—"

"Bring the doctor, madam." His father, always the portrait of tact and kindness, interrupted the nurse.

She frowned and squared her shoulders. "The doctor will come once the patient has his breakfast. And only one family member may be present in the room." She raised her brows, daring his father to protest.

Inappropriate laughter simmered in Gabriel's throat at the shocked expression on his father's face. Nobody spoke to his father that way.

"We're so sorry. We've just arrived from France. I shall stay and my husband and daughter will step outside. Do you have a lounge or waiting area please?" His beautiful elegant mother soothed the ruffled feathers.

Like she always had to do when her ruthless husband offended someone. Which was on a daily, oh hell—on an hourly basis.

His father opened his mouth to object, but Claude clasped his arm. "Come Papa, we'll go see how this hospital coffee tastes." She wrinkled her nose, winked at Gabriel, and pulled their father away.

Dr. Reynolds entered the room with another physician, a tall, slender ebony-skinned woman.

"Mr. DuVernay," Dr. Reynolds nodded at him. "This is Dr. Odhiambo and she is one of the top orthopedic surgeons in the country. We've been discussing your case." He shifted his gaze toward his mom.

"Hello. You can call me Gabriel. This is my mother, Michele Gaillard DuVernay." Gabriel's blood thrummed and his pulse hammered in his temples.

"Well Gabriel, we've discussed your case and also spoken with Dr. Davidson at the Kerlan-Jobe clinic." Dr. Odhiambo paused, her dark eyes sympathetic. "There are a few options to discuss."

Gabriel nodded, his ears humming now. A surreal type of cloud settled around him. Like he was in the room with them, but somehow behind some kind of veil. He managed a curt nod, every muscle in his body tightening in anticipation. His maman laid one cool slender hand on his shoulder and squeezed. He exhaled, comforted by her presence and her strength.

"Well, I'll be frank. Your patella is broken into numerous pieces. Your ACL, MCL, and meniscus are all torn." Her voice was crisp and clear.

Gabriel's mother flinched and her grip deepened on his shoulder. An icy numbness spread along his skin until he couldn't feel his own face or fingers or feet. He must have nodded because the doctor continued.

"We don't think your patella can be repaired without putting in some metal plates to fortify the joint. We recommend the next surgery do this and also repair the tendons and ligaments as much as possible. You will most likely need more hardware to reattach the tendons. Rehabilitation will take anywhere from three to nine months. The other option is a total knee replacement." Her words dropped like a death knell.

At least she didn't smile or try to soften the blow.

The buzzing in his ears intensified into a thundering roar, the peaceful sea from his dream transforming into angry waves slamming against unforgiving cliffs. He opened his mouth, and then clicked his jaw shut.

"Will he be able to return to the game?" His mother asked in her measured, melodic English.

The doctors must be experts in delivering shitty news because neither of them flinched. They glanced at each other. "The odds of returning to the game are slim. I'm sorry." Dr. Reynolds' quiet words sliced through his heart like a machete.

For a moment the room was silent. The weight of the news hung like an anvil, ready to fall and crush them all. Hell, it had already dropped. He recoiled back against the pillows and groaned.

He'd never play soccer again.

"Are you sure?" The words slipped through his frozen lips, despite knowing the answer. These doctors knew who he was. Knew their local team paid a king's ransom bringing him to California. They were damn sure.

"Gabriel, we'll have the best surgeons in the country operate on your knee. Every state-of-the-art technique and machine possible for rehabilitation. But playing soccer on a professional level?" Dr. Odhiambo's brows knit together.

"You won't be offended if we seek another opinion, correct?" His maman asked.

Gabriel's mind whirled. *Done. Finished.* He was only thirty-one years old. He clenched his hands into fists and slammed one against the metal railing of his bed, welcoming the sharp burst of pain. Wanting to feel anything but this horrible deadness permeating his body and his mind. Filling him with a black void of nothingness.

He'd never play soccer again.

His life was over. Gabriel dropped his head back on the pillows and closed his eyes, only darkness behind his lids now. Why couldn't he *feel* anything?

Dr. Odhiambo said, "We know this is terrible news and a shock. Of course you can consult with whomever you wish, but you'll want to have surgery sooner than later."

"Can we bring him home until it is time for the next operation? We can hire a nurse or whatever staff necessary."

The doctors looked at each other. "Usually, he would remain here because the surgery needs to happen this week. But, yes, he can be accommodated at home." Because we know you have the money. The unsaid words hung in the air.

"Thank you." His mother said.

"Of course. Should we send in your father and sister now?"

"Non," his mother snapped, her poised demeanor slipping a bit. "I will fetch them. We need a few minutes alone."

They exited, quietly pulling the door closed behind them.

"Gabriel. Look at me." Her tone was urgent. Hushed.

He forced himself to open his eyes. Her expression was fierce, her eyes hot, and her jaw hard. "Everything will work out. We'll figure this out."

"Maman, my career is finished. *Fini*. It's all I ever wanted." He clenched the sheets, seeking some feeling to surface. Any feeling at all.

If only he could sink back into his dream. Or now simply sink underneath the water never to surface from the depths.

His maman switched to French. "We must make

a plan before your papa returns. I know football is your first love. This is tragic and terrible and if I could take away the pain I would do this for you. My heart breaks for you. But I cannot change this. You must face that you'll never play again." Her large gray eyes burned with grief.

The truth in her words washed over him. "Plans? My life is over." Self-pity filled him and he didn't care. Fuck it.

"Your papa will try to force you to return home to Sablet immediately. To begin assuming the lead role at the winery so he can retire." She squeezed his hand.

"But I had until I was thirty-five, I–" Panic pulsed in his chest.

"Everything is different now. We need a new plan to persuade your father that your sister wants to run the winery. Deserves to run it. We don't have years to convince him anymore." Her voice brooked no dissent.

"You're right. Claude has the best palate, the best skills in the fields, has her sommelier status, and the respect of every single vineyard employee. Why can't he see that?" His maman was right. His dad would steamroll all of them.

She shook her head. "It drives me crazy too. Your father is a good man, you know this, but he is old-fashioned. His father hammered it into his head that the eldest son needs to run the family business, just like they've done for the last two centuries. Despite many of the top wine houses being run by women. So we must plan."

"I could just tell him no." Even as he uttered the words, he knew he could not. Much as he disagreed with his father's antiquated ideas, he was a DuVernay and he'd always known he had to have *some* part in the business.

But now he'd tasted freedom, true freedom. Time, he needed more time.

"I'm sure that would work as well as every other discussion the two of you have had in this regard. No, we need to be smart. And if you and your sister and I can work together, we'll manage it." She stroked his hair back from his forehead, a gesture reminiscent from when he was a boy. "I'll do my best to keep him focused on the immediate–that we need to support you through the surgery and rehabilitation. Under no circumstances will he discuss the succession until your health is assured."

His mother used to fix everything when he was a child. Wouldn't it be nice if she could do it now too? It all seemed surreal. Yesterday, he was the top soccer star in the world, on track to breaking every single scoring record. Hell, ESPN wanted to film a documentary about him. And now?

He'd never play soccer again.

"I need to talk to my coach. I'm not sure if he's done a press release now or what they are telling the media. We cannot say anything yet. Nothing at all." He grimaced.

"Of course not, but the paparazzi are swarming downstairs. Does anybody else know the truth about your injury?" Her mouth turned down.

Gabriel's heart thawed and he nodded. "Yes,

actually she was here for me yesterday." Dylan. He looked around for his phone so he could text her.

"A woman? Can she be trusted? You need to be careful in your position…" One winged brow arched.

"In my position what? It's not like I'll be famous much longer. We met in Paris last year and she isn't interested in the press. Please give me my phone." He wasn't going to let his parents and his situation control every move he made from here forward. Damn it.

"Hmmm…how can you be sure?"

"I'm sure, okay? You'd like her. She's an artist."

"Do I know her work?" Her steel gray eyes narrowed, but she handed him the phone.

He shook his head and scrolled through the messages. Some of his buddies from his former team Barcelona had reached out. He'd deal with them later. A couple guys from the Galaxy had also texted. A text from the coach asking him to call when he woke up.

Ah, there it was—a text from Dylan— and somehow the dark cloud lightened. His shoulders softened and his lips curved up. Suddenly a sliver of hope appeared.

CHAPTER 7

DYLAN SMOOTHED DOWN THE IRIS-COL-ORED cotton skirt of her favorite sundress. Her pulse hammered in her throat. All her senses were tuned in to the salty scent of the ocean so close to Gabriel's door, to the crispness of the early evening breeze, to the bumping of kids on their skateboards cruising along the boardwalk. She'd parked a few blocks from Gabriel's sleek, modern white corner condo. No press in sight, thank goodness.

Pausing at the security gate, she took a few cleansing breaths and tapped the buzzer. The tall barrier silently slid open. She ascended the polished stone steps to his metallic silver door. His home resembled one of the newer modern villas you'd find in the South of France. The exterior was as gorgeous as what she'd seen of the interior. Before she could knock, the door opened.

A tall woman with close-cropped ash blonde hair, unusual ice gray eyes, and patrician features greeted her in a lilting accent. "Hello, you must be Dylan?"

"Yes, I mean oui, I'm Dylan McNeill." She

stammered her response in French, cursing the surge of anxiety rushing through her body.

"Please come in. I am Gabriel's mother, Michele." She stepped to the side, and Dylan entered the spacious airy room.

Gabriel was sitting on the enormous navy sofa, with his leg propped up on several colorful throw pillows. A contraption was wrapped around his knee and attached to what appeared to be a cooler with a long corrugated hose. His face lit up when he saw her and despite his sleepy gaze, he looked heartbreakingly handsome, especially with his wide smile.

Her tummy took a long slow roll as she crossed the room. This guy was irresistible, even as an injured soldier. Something about him pulled at her heartstrings. "How are you?"

He shrugged. "I've been better, but at least I'm out of the hospital."

She knelt next to the couch so she wasn't looming over him. "Anything I can do?"

His bottle green eyes crinkled at the corners and he shook his head. Now that she was closer she noticed the pallor beneath his olive skin and the strained lines bracketing his mouth. "Just glad you came. You look beautiful." His voice was low and raspy.

Devastatingly sexy.

"So, your family is here?" Her stiff shoulders softened. She'd tossed and turned last night, worried for him. He'd just lost his ultimate dream of helping elevate his sport in the U.S. to compete with the rest of the world. Wouldn't distancing herself from him be simpler now? Less like she was abandoning him when he was down. Now she'd seen the way the press mobbed him, she couldn't risk experiencing that nightmare again. So why did her heart ache?

He nodded. "My father and sister flew back today, but my mother's staying for the next surgery."

"I was about to open a bottle of wine and get some supper. Why don't you peruse the menu and send in the dinner order?" Michele said as she strolled to Gabriel's wine fridge in the kitchen.

Dylan turned and caught Michele's gaze. "Anything I can do?" She pushed to her feet and picked up the tablet from the coffee table.

"We've already put in our choices, so just add yours. I hope Thai is okay." Gabriel murmured. He looked so sweet despite the pain and the gravity of his situation.

"I love Thai." She moved to the leather armchair next to the couch, added Tom Yum Soup, and hit send.

Once Gabriel's mother handed Dylan and Gabriel their wineglasses, she sat in the other armchair and studied them. Dylan worked not to squirm in her seat.

"So my son tells me you're an artist. Did Gabriel tell you I'm a patron of the arts? I use my maiden name, Gaillard. What's your medium?" Michele smiled.

Gaillard? Of course Dylan had heard of her–she

was internationally famous.

"I'm a painter. Oil and watercolor mostly. Landscapes and portraits set in nature with a classical impressionistic bent and a modern edge." Dylan sipped her wine and tried to relax.

"Have I seen your work anywhere? I love portraits." Michele's tilted her elegant head.

Dylan gulped and shook her head. If only she could claim some famous galleries. After sixty-plus rejections, it was tough to stay positive. But his mom didn't need to know that. Nor did Gabriel for that matter. She'd even hidden her fear of failure from her own family.

She pasted a bright smile on her face. "Not yet. I'm hoping to have an exhibition down in Laguna Beach very soon."

"That's lovely. Gabriel said you met in Paris. Did you study there?" Michele's poker face rivaled her older sister Amanda's.

Dylan swallowed and squared her shoulders. A poker face was not her specialty. Heat began to rise up her neck and she peeked over at Gabriel. He was fiddling with the pack on his leg, his brow furrowed.

"Yes, I did study in Paris back in college for a semester. It's my favorite city. Last summer, I was visiting my best friend." *And picked up your handsome son in a bar.* She stuck her nose in the berry red wine and inhaled.

"Mmm, the wine smells so delicious. Is it one of the DuVernay GSM blends?" Everyone knew the DuVernays were pioneers in the popular blend from the Southern Rhone Valley. Discussing wine was safer than discussing the night she and Gabriel met.

Before his mom could respond, Gabriel said, "Yes, it's a 2010, one of the best vintages we've had. I was saving it for a special occasion…"

Dylan smiled. "Yes, your mom is here, so that's a special occasion, right?"

His sculpted lips quirked up and he shrugged.

"My darling, being here with you and meeting your friend is a special occasion. Bien sur. So where did you two meet? At a museum or gallery?" Michele lifted her glass.

Dylan tucked a strand of hair behind her ear and swallowed to moisten the desert now inhabiting her throat. Her mind blanked and she looked at Gabriel to save her from humiliating herself.

"We met through some mutual friends, Maman, just out on a lovely summer Paris night." He reached one tanned hand over and clasped hers.

"I don't mean to pry, but was one of the reasons you accepted the Los Angeles' team offer because of Dylan?" Her eyes narrowed as she continued to look between them.

A laugh gurgled out before she could prevent it. *Oh my god.* Dylan sank a little in her seat. Her cheeks flamed—her fair complexion never failed to betray her embarrassment. "Um—"

"Maman, you are distressing my guest. But non, I accepted the Galaxy's offer because it was the best. Not that it matters now." He slammed his wineglass onto the coffee table.

"Gabriel, I am sorry. There's a reason I'm asking these questions. Does Dylan know about the winery and your obligations?"

Gabriel sucked in a sharp inhale. "Maman."

"Well?" One delicate golden brow arched.

Gabriel glanced at Dylan. "Oui, I mentioned how Claude should take over our winery business when the time comes and how I'd rather remain here. There's no need to burden her with the family drama."

"I have an idea. It's unorthodox, but it might work." Michele's eyes gleamed silver now. "How much do you want your art out in the world? In major galleries worldwide?"

Dylan jolted. "Excuse me?" She looked at Gabriel and his face looked bewildered too.

"Maman?" His eyes were wide.

Michele held up two elegant pale hands. "Perhaps you two could make an arrangement and buy some time for Claude to prove herself and for you to make a plan, Gabriel."

"Arrangement?" Gabriel asked.

"Arrangement?" Dylan echoed.

Michele nodded. "Let me explain. Your papa will push you to return immediately to run the winery now that your football career is ending. We knew the day would come, but I assumed Claude would have stepped in by then. I know your injury seems like the end of the world, but perhaps now we can show a different reason for you to remain here in California."

Dylan looked between Gabriel's shocked

expression and his mother's now animated one, completely at sea.

"If you two get engaged, you can say you must remain here to not just fully recuperate, but to live with your fiancé while she pursues her dreams. That will give us the breathing room to find another solution without battling against your father now. It will also give Claude the opportunity to kick up her efforts and prove herself. She's working on a new rosé that could be a huge success. It's a perfect solution." She smiled a smug grin.

"Engaged? I'm sorry, but I don't understand." Understatement of the century. Was his mom playing with a full deck?

Gabriel barked out a laugh. "Maman, have you been drinking? Neither of us is in the position to get married, we just started seeing each other."

Michele frowned. "You said you met in Paris a year ago. You haven't seen each other until you arrived here? I've seen the way you look at each other and I assumed–"

Heat rose in Dylan's cheeks again. His mother was too observant. "We met in Paris, but no. We just really started seeing each other so an engagement is out of the question."

His mother sliced her hand through the air. "Bah, It doesn't matter. It would be a business arrangement. Six months and then you would both be free. Gabriel would buy time to figure out an alternate plan of what he wants to do and give his sister the chance to prove herself. I will also be working on my husband to see reason during this time."

She turned her attention to Dylan. "For you, I will connect you with my contacts here and in Europe if you wish. You will have the chance to prove yourself by getting exhibitions. It's a win-win."

Dylan's pulse accelerated and wild thoughts zipped around her brain. Maybe Gabriel's mother was certifiably off her rocker, but some of it actually made sense. At least on her end. Michele's influence, mentorship, and assistance for six months could propel her career forward in ways she could only dream of. If she'd asked her dad, he'd simply call in favors and she'd never know if her work had been accepted on its own merit. Michele Gaillard's recommendations carried weight.

She shook her head—no way could she fake getting married. "I'm not really sure I'm the right person for this. My family wouldn't believe I'd gone and suddenly gotten engaged, for one thing." Although, she could say that they'd been corresponding in secret since Paris and she just didn't want to tell anyone.

She clasped her hands together and squeezed. Was she actually considering this madcap plan? Was he? She looked at Gabriel, who was leaning his head back against the pillows, and pinching the bridge of his nose between his fingers.

"Are you in pain? Can I get you anything?" Dylan forgot about his mom for a moment.

His eyes opened and he grinned wryly. "I feel like I'm in some weird alternate universe because what my maman is suggesting actually makes perfect sense to me. But then I know my father. Would you consider it?" His gaze sharpened on hers.

Dylan gulped. "It just sounds like something on a soap opera or a bad TV movie, you know? Who pretends to be engaged?"

"Well, we'd get to spend more time together." Again, that devastating smile. "You'd gain exposure without having to rely on your family. I could have some breathing room to get better and make a plan. It could be fun." His smile grew a hint more wicked.

Perspiration prickled on the back of Dylan's neck. Fun? "I mean, how would this even work?"

Even though she'd be lying if she denied feeling excited at the prospect of being with Gabriel day and night for half a year. In the short amount of time they'd spent together, he'd stirred deep emotions within her heart. So, she'd probably fall madly in love with him and be heartbroken when he sailed off after the arrangement ended.

Michele pounced. "You are considering it, yes? Well, I think nobody needs to know you haven't been corresponding and even seeing each other in secret over the last year, oui?" She nodded and continued without waiting for their response.

"It's all very romantic. And now Gabriel's injury just made you two realize how in love you are and that you want to make this commitment now because you never know what will happen next. It will also help take the attention off of Gabriel."

"But what about all the women you've been photographed with over the last year? Why would you be seen with them if you've secretly been in love with me?" Dylan frowned—what if her family had seen them?

"Gabriel?" His mother glared at him.

Gabriel winced. "Look, I can't control all the photos. Most of them were fan selfies or just casual dates to events I had to attend. There hasn't been another girlfriend or relationship. You know how the media sensationalizes everything—it's not real."

Crap, the paparazzi. "Well, actually I'm sorry but I don't think I can do it. I can't live a public life like that." Dylan shook her head. Too much exposure.

The temptation of exhibitions and opportunity had pulled her away from the reality of all the publicity involved with being Gabriel's fiancé. Her sisters would hate it and so would she.

"But if your art is indeed good and you gain a reputation, you will have publicity." Michele frowned again.

"It's not the same. Nobody chases artists. But Gabriel is a huge star, like my parents were. I'm sorry." Dylan's stomach dropped. It was impossible.

"Well, hold on." Gabriel scrubbed his hands through his thick brown hair and squeezed his eyes shut. "After the Galaxy dumps me, I'll be out of the news. Old news. Nobody will care what I'm doing if I'm not playing."

"Gabriel." Dylan touched his shoulder again and smiled gently. "You are more than just a soccer player."

"Just a soccer player? Are you kidding me?" He exploded, grief morphing into fury. "Football is everything to me. Everything. And now it is gone. And I am correct that nobody will give a shit. I'll be old news and the stories will dwindle down to past history."

She scooted back in her chair. He was more than just the game of soccer, even if he couldn't see that now. And it wasn't her place to try to explain that to him, especially one day after his dreams shattered and he was in significant pain–medication and ice machine notwithstanding. Her heart ached for him.

"Gabriel. Enough. Of course you are devastated, my son. I think Dylan meant your career and your status are just part of who you are. I'm just trying to buy you more time to figure out what to do next." Her voice was soft.

She turned to Dylan. "If I could use my influence to minimize the press attention, would you still consider it? There are measures we could take to keep Gabriel out of the public eye."

Dylan hesitated–she'd squashed the lifeline his mom offered. But if she and her family weren't subjected to unwanted scrutiny? Was there a way? An idea popped into her brain.

A totally ridiculous idea.

As if this entire plot wasn't preposterous enough already. But how outlandish would it be? She'd need her late mother's acting skills to pull it off.

"Well, I do have an idea for more privacy. I just don't know if it would work and if you could handle it." Dylan nibbled on her lower lip.

"I've handled a lot. What's your idea?" Gabriel arched a dark brow.

"Well, my father moved us to Pacific Vista Ranch after my mother died because the paparazzi made our life impossible—I'm talking Princess Diana level of stalking—and our ranch is very secluded. If we did do this, and I'm not saying I agree to it, but if we did do this, we could stay at the ranch and that way we'd avoid all the issues we'd have here in L.A."

Gabriel frowned. "But my place here on the beach…"

His mother interrupted. "You don't need to live in this place on the beach. It would be good for you to get out of the spotlight anyway. You would have to let the press know you're engaged though. It does need to look legitimate for your father. You know he is traditional. But we could keep a limit on the details."

Gabriel threw up his hands. "And what the hell will I do on a ranch? Become a cowboy?"

Dylan narrowed her eyes. "No. It's a two hundred and twenty acre horse-breeding ranch five miles from the beach, not the movie set of a spaghetti western. You could heal and figure out what's next—isn't that the entire point of this scheme?"

"Gabriel, control your temper. You need to focus on recovery and figure out your next career move. Otherwise, your father won't stop until you return to Sablet." His mother scolded.

Dylan shot to her feet and paced over to the closed glass doors leading to the deck and the freedom of the ocean breeze outside. This was madness. She gazed out at the darkening sky, her mind whirling and her stomach in knots.

She whirled to face them. Gabriel stared morosely down at his leg. His mother gulped her wine. Probably not a common occurrence. A familiar desperate urge to flee overcame her—no way could she make such a momentous decision with the two of them pressuring her.

She strode to the couch and looked down at the most gorgeous complicated man she'd ever met. "Look, I need some time to digest all of this. I'll give you my answer tomorrow, okay?"

He reached for her hand and tugged her closer. "Are you sure? Won't you at least stay for dinner?"

"I'm not hungry. Sorry. Gabriel, I've got to go. I'll call you tomorrow." Her voice softened.

His mom had to have sprung this proposition on them both, unless he was an Oscar-worthy actor. She loosened his grip and stepped back.

She hurried toward the door, not caring if her pace was close to a run. If she didn't get out of here, she might combust.

CHAPTER 8

GABRIEL GROANED AND PUNCHED THE couch cushion. Managed not to curse and hurl his wineglass against the pristine white walls of his condo. The fateful moment he'd taken attention away from the ball replayed on a loop in his mind. Why had he done it?

Because his damn ego had been so inflated and he'd basked in the admiration.

Because he'd believed himself to be invincible.

Because he'd already cemented his status in the world record books for most goals. Not to mention the most lucrative financial deal in football history.

Yesterday morning he was on top of the world and now he was considering a fake engagement with Dylan at the behest of his mother. Like it was a reasonable solution, no less. What the actual hell?

"It's insane, Maman. Now Dylan's run away and who knows if she'll come back." At all for any reason. Ever.

His mom crossed the room and perched on the edge of the chair next to him. "Gabriel, I know it's extreme, but I think it could work. Think of your freedom. And aren't you willing to do anything for a chance to help Claude?"

"But even if your idea worked, is an engagement reason enough for me to stay here?" He stared over his mother's shoulder at the black sky outside.

"Gabriel, *attention*," his mother snapped.

Gabriel forced himself to meet his mother's gaze and listen.

"Your father would understand your desire to be with your future wife, especially while you recuperate. Think of it as hitting the pause button long enough to delay your father's pig-headedness." She leaned in and brushed his hair back from his face, her smile wistful.

She continued, "Claude can accelerate her efforts on the new vintage. It will give you time to adjust from the shock of what has happened. It will give us all time." Her jaw clicked shut, her "brook no argument" façade fully in place.

Shock was right. He kneaded the back of his neck, which felt more like granite than muscle and bone. "But live on a ranch with Dylan's family? To convince them we've been seeing each other secretly for a year and that we're really getting married?"

"Well, I believed you were enamored when she arrived, they will too. Being somewhere secluded is a positive, no? You'll want to be away from the press too. It's the perfect solution. And if I know you, it won't be such a hardship. She's very beautiful." Her smile was smug.

He dropped his head back on the couch cushions again. All his dreams were shattered, just like his leg. Not that he could feel his knee in the wall of ice surrounding it.

"Gabriel?"

"Oui, she is beautiful and fascinating and special. But it doesn't change the rest of it. If Papa finds out we've all gone behind his back, all hell will break loose. And the way Dylan sprinted out of here, who knows if she will agree." Gabriel's knee throbbed and his head pounded.

"Well, if she truly wants her career to take off, she will agree. I hope her work is worthy. But even if it isn't, there are many who will do me a favor."

Gabriel shrugged. "She wants to prove herself and although I haven't seen her paintings, she's passionate and has an artist's soul. I have a gut feeling she's talented and just needs the chance." So much for them developing a natural relationship now, though.

"Look, I know it's not ordinary, but nothing about these circumstances is ordinary. I want to help you and Claude. You two are my priority." Urgency colored his mother's voice.

"Even if it means deceiving your husband? Even over the DuVernay legacy?" How far would his mother go and how would it impact his parent's marriage?

She flicked her hand again. "This is for the DuVernay legacy. Your sister was born to run the winery and she will. You will figure out your next steps. We just need six months. Your father will come to see reason eventually. Give Dylan time to think about it. I can sweeten the pot by providing the names of some prestigious galleries where I can get her in, if more details will help."

"Let's just see what she says." Not that spending time with Dylan would be a hardship, but dating exclusively and marriage were too different animals.

The doorbell rang and his mom rose and crossed the room to fetch their meal. How different than the other night when he and Dylan had shared a romantic meal. *Zut.*

For now, there was nothing for him to do but wait to hear from his doctors, his coach, his manager, and Dylan. Nothing was certain any longer.

"Allo?" Gabriel answered the phone without looking at the screen. He was still groggy from the pain meds he'd taken at 3 a.m. to combat the excruciating pain.

"Gabriel? It's Suzanne, Dr. Odhiambo's scheduler. She would like to move forward with your surgery first thing tomorrow morning."

Gabriel shifted back up onto the stacked pillows and cursed at the immediate jolt of pain up his leg. "Tomorrow?"

"Yes, surgery at 7 a.m. tomorrow and pre-op today at 11 a.m."

He exhaled. "Do I have a choice?"

In Gabriel's past experience with minor medical issues, the schedulers usually worked around his schedule and offered options. But apparently when your knee was destroyed, they knew your calendar was wide open. Yet another sign he was screwed.

"Mr. DuVernay?" Suzanne's voice was high.

He shook his head. She was just doing her job and didn't need his foul mood foisted upon her. "Yes. I will be there."

He glanced down at his phone. It was already 8:45 a.m. and it would probably take him an hour to take a damned shower.

Gabriel ended the call and flopped back onto the bed and stared at the ceiling. Was this nightmare going to be his life for the foreseeable future? But maybe the surgeons could perform a miracle. He managed to get out of bed and used the crutches to hobble into the bathroom. He heard his mom out in the kitchen. At least she was here.

Shower first. Maybe it would help him feel less like a miserable beast. Yeah, right.

Fortunately, his shower was equipped with a built-in bench. He'd imagined sharing it with Dylan, not because he couldn't stand long enough to shampoo his hair. He showered and only slipped twice. Now he knew why old people dreaded the shower—it was a goddamn landmine full of ways to slip and break every bone in your body. He yanked on some baggy shorts and a t-shirt and crutched his way into the kitchen.

"You're up and showered. Good. I've made coffee and the skillet is ready for your eggs. Sunny side up as usual?" His mother's tone was cheerful and brisk, like it was any other morning.

For some reason, it put his teeth on edge. "You sound cheerful this morning."

Her brow creased and she poured some coffee and gave him the cup. "Have some coffee. It will help. Have you heard from your doctors?"

He accepted the drink and sipped. Ah, his Maman brewed the coffee deep and black, which suited his mood. Perfect. "Oui. Pre-op today at 11 a.m. and surgery at 7 tomorrow."

She nodded and turned back to the stove. "The sooner the better. Isn't that what your doctor said at the hospital? Okay, I will take you."

Gabriel sat and drank his coffee until his mother slid the plate of eggs in front of him. "Merci."

"Have you heard from Dylan?"

"Non." He shook his head. After the way she'd bolted out of the apartment last night, he figured she needed time to make up her mind.

"Well, if you haven't heard from her, I'd call her later today to tell her about the surgery. If you two are going to be engaged, she will need to be by your bedside. And you'll also have to figure out how soon you can move down to the ranch to recuperate. The sooner the better."

Gabriel dropped his head into his hands. It was all too much too fast. How could he think of the long-term with this surgery looming over him? He'd only planned for one thing in his life and it was finished. A little time to adjust would be nice.

His mom patted his shoulder. "It will all work out. It may not appear that way now, but I feel it. Just focus on getting well quickly."

He reached back and squeezed her hand. Right now he just needed to keep his shit together before heading to the hospital. No time to contemplate how the rest of life looked like he was leaping off a cliff into the unknown.

CHAPTER 9

DYLAN DISMOUNTED FROM HER HORSE
Lacy and dropped the reins. The sky was
pure blue, the rolling hills dotted with chestnut
and brown and black horses lazily munching away.
They'd ridden to one of her sweet mare's favorite
spots, a verdant bluff at the far end of the ranch
overlooking the sprawling pastures. She spread out
the soft plaid blanket on the green grass warmed
from the early morning sun, and then unpacked
her art supplies.

Drawing helped quiet her mind and settle her
overactive nerves. Time to disengage from the
anxiety and dramatic repetitive thoughts circling
around her brain or risk shrieking like a wild
monkey. Pacific Vista Ranch was both heaven
and haven. Would the haven still feel like a refuge
if she brought Gabriel here under false pretenses?

She tucked her legs beneath her and flipped
open the sketchbook to a blank page and brought
pencil to paper. Her thoughts flew as swiftly as
her fingers across the cream-colored sheet. Had
she lost her last marble because somehow she was
seriously considering Gabriel's mother's unortho-

dox proposal?

A sham engagement. Just as Gabriel's father's expectations for him to be heir and take over the winery seemed anachronistic to her, so did the idea of a marriage of convenience. They weren't living in a nineteenth-century novel. And they'd have to convince her family and his father and the world, for that matter, that their relationship was authentic.

No denying their explosive chemistry, but a quick engagement out of the blue would be tough for anyone to accept. And the dangerous fact remained she could actually fall in love with him. For real.

Because she was attracted to Gabriel. Because she'd kept other guys at arm's length since their passionate night together last summer. Because her heart had galloped against her ribs when she'd received his text invitation to his game. Because every nerve and cell and her body fired and came alive when they kissed on his balcony last week.

The charcoal continued stroking over the page, her fingers moving along almost of their own volition. Something shifted in her chest.

She glanced back down at her sketchpad and gasped. She'd drawn Gabriel's proud, handsome profile, just as she'd seen him that first night in Paris. Just as she'd admired the other night when she sat next to him. Just as she'd sketched several times before in the last year. Granted, she'd tucked those pictures away where nobody would discover them.

Yes, she was attracted to him and afraid she could fall in love with him and have her heart smashed to pieces at the end of their six-month bargain.

Her phone rang and Gabriel's name popped up on the screen. Her fingers trembled as she accepted the call.

"Hello." Her pulse quickened.

"Dylan?" Gabriel's mother asked.

Dylan jolted. "Hello Michele, is Gabriel okay?" What if he'd taken a turn for the worse?

"Oui. He is doing his pre-op now. Surgery is scheduled for first thing tomorrow morning. Have you made your decision yet?" His mother's voice was melodic and firm.

Dylan exhaled unsteadily. "Well, I'd like to have this discussion with Gabriel if you don't mind. But yes, I've made my decision."

Dylan gazed down at the picture she'd drawn of Gabriel. Soon she'd be seeing that face every single day. And night. She sucked in another deep breath and held it. A few moments ticked away in silence.

"I understand, but can you at least tell me yes or no?"

Sweat beaded on her brow and her upper lip. "Yes, I'm going to do it. But, as I mentioned, I want to discuss details with Gabriel first. I hope you understand." Could she live a fake life in order to achieve her dreams?

Michele sighed. "Thank you so much. You have no idea how much this will help our family. Help

Gabriel."

Dylan's shoulders softened and the knots in her belly loosened. "Well, I'm not selfless and not doing it just to help Gabriel. I'm taking the risk of hurting my family because I'm at a turning point in my life too. This bargain needs to be reciprocal."

"Of course, of course. Don't worry about that. I can get you the appointments and even encourage the exhibitions. You understand if your art isn't well-received, however, there's nothing I can do," Michele said.

Dylan stared out over the rolling grassy hills. "I just want the opportunity. I wouldn't want to achieve the success on any other basis than my own talent."

Which is why she'd never asked her dad to pull in favors with his contacts. Now, she'd finally have exhibitions, but would the world laud her accomplishments? Or if she bombed on a big stage, would her career begin and end the same day? Agreeing to this mad scheme would accelerate everything and any safety net would evaporate into thin air. Imposter syndrome was no joke.

"Well, Gabriel should be out in about fifteen minutes. Perhaps you can call him then. And can you arrange to be here for his surgery tomorrow? I think the sooner you are with him, especially in this terrible time in his life, the more legitimate your relationship will appear." Michele was obviously used to being in charge.

Dylan squeezed her eyes closed. She could do

this. "I can definitely be there. We'll also have some planning to do—when to tell my family, when to announce it to the press, moving Gabriel here once he's able to do so, prepping my work for exhibition…"

Her gut clenched. My god, what was she embarking on? Nothing would ever be the same again once they started down this path.

"Don't get too worried. I will be able to coordinate a lot of this for you two. Ah, hold on."

"Dylan?" Gabriel's gravelly voice came onto the phone.

"Hi Gabriel." *My fiancé.*

"Are you doing okay today?" He sounded subdued.

Her heart kicked against her ribs. He was preparing for a grueling life-changing surgery and he was asking about her first. "I'm fine. More importantly, how are you? Your mother said surgery is tomorrow?"

"You spoke with my maman?"

Damn. Well, they'd be lying to their family, friends, and the entire world for that matter, so they better get in the habit of being honest with each other. "Yes, she called me right before I was about to call you."

"Ah. I thought you'd called."

"She beat me to it. I've made my decision, Gabriel. I will do it. What's next?" The words whooshed out.

He exhaled. "Oh, thank god. Will you come up tonight?"

Here we go. "Yes, I can do that. What about your coach and manager and the team? Have you met with them yet? Is there a plan with what to tell the press?"

"Later today. There will be a press release about me having surgery and I think they'll keep it vague." His voice was raspy now, barely audible.

"Okay, but I need to prepare my family and I think it would be best if we told them before there is any announcement of the engagement. I'll need to make sure we can move into the guesthouse as soon as you can." The flutters in her belly morphed into quaking. Neither of their lives would ever be the same.

He hesitated for a minute. "My manager and PR person will make sure to control the story."

"Okay. Of course." Her eyes filled with tears and her heart ached for Gabriel. His dream career gone in a flash. Whether their engagement would be newsworthy or important solely for his own purposes remained to be seen.

His voice lowered to a whisper. "All anybody will really care about is that the Galaxy spent a fortune on me, whether they'll have to pay me, and who can try to replace me."

"Nobody could replace you. I'm so sorry, Gabriel. I know this is devastating." Hell, she'd met Gabriel because she'd been distraught over her own family's tragic past being resurrected. The press would leap on the story of the Galaxy losing their star recruit and he'd have to relive it for a long time.

"We'll see. We'll get the engagement news out so my father knows. Again, you do need to prepare your family."

Dylan nodded and gazed out into the clear sunny day. "I will. This should be interesting." What if they spent the next half a year together and fell in love?

"It will work out. I must go now. When will I see you? I've got a guest room if you'd like to stay and accompany me to the hospital."

She sighed. Would they share a bed when he moved to Pacific Vista Ranch, for real or even for appearances? Her belly kicked again. "Okay. I'll tell my family this afternoon and then come up this evening. Good luck with your meeting."

"Thank you Dylan. Au revoir."

"Au revoir." She closed her eyes and swallowed the lump in her throat. Time to channel her mom's thespian abilities.

CHAPTER 10

DYLAN DRUMMED HER FINGERS ON the enormous pale granite island and glanced at the kitchen clock for the tenth time. She'd requested a family meeting for 4 p.m. and it was already 3:58 without a sign of anyone, not even her stepmom, Angela, who was always early. Dylan hadn't initiated a family meeting in about a decade, when she went off to Valencia for art school. You'd think everyone would actually show up.

She practiced her stress relief breathing technique, inhaling for four, holding for four, and exhaling for four, as slowly as she could. Her family teased her for wearing her heart on her sleeve and today she'd have to convince them she was over the moon in love with Gabriel. So madly in love she'd hidden it for a year and gotten engaged without telling them.

She jumped when a hand landed on her shoulder. She turned her head and smiled up into her beloved father's ruggedly handsome face. "There you are."

"Sorry, I couldn't get off this phone call. Everything okay? You haven't asked us to get together this way for years." His hazel eyes crinkled at the corners and he gently squeezed her shoulder.

"Yes, everything is fine. I just have some news and wanted to share it all at the same time." Dylan's nerves began thrumming beneath the surface of her skin.

She stepped away from her dad and opened the large stainless steel refrigerator and pulled out a pitcher of mint iced tea. "Let's sit. I already got out glasses for everyone." Mint was supposed to be soothing, right?

Raised voices signaled the rest of the family's approach. Sam and her husband Holt were arguing about something—usually foreplay for them because they just loved to kiss and make up. Amanda and Jake and Angela were obviously talking about something else because their voices were normal inside voices level. Life was status quo for the McNeill clan.

Everyone but her.

Dylan glanced up and smiled as the rest of her family entered the kitchen and took a seat around the table. Angela returned her smile, her eyes questioning, yet reassuring as always. Beads of perspiration popped up on the back of her neck. She could do this. She *would* do this. She'd made a deal and McNeills *always* kept their deals.

She swallowed a sip of the cool liquid to soothe the parched desert that was now her throat. "Well, I've got some news and you all may be surprised because, well, I haven't been very forthcoming with you about something really important." She exhaled. Not a bad start.

"You got an exhibition?" Sam demanded, leaning forward in her seat.

"There's some progress on that front, but the real news is a little more personal." She paused and smoothed a strand of hair away from her now overheated forehead. "It's about Gabriel, the soccer player I met in France last summer."

"The one whose knee just got blown out?" Holt asked, his brows drawn together. He had probably broken most of the bones in his body during his stuntman career.

"You went up to see him at the hospital afterward, right?" Amanda asked, threading her fingers through Jake's on the table.

"Have I heard of this guy? You met him in Paris?" Her father's eyes widened.

Dylan nodded and held up her hands to stave off the barrage. "Yes, Gabriel DuVernay. He recently got a huge contract with the L.A. Galaxy."

Jake whistled through his teeth. "Yeah, he's like the best player in the world and L.A. paid hundreds of millions for him."

"What's the important news, honey?" Her stepmom encouraged.

Her family was staring at her, waiting for her to continue. Adrenaline kicked through her veins. *Respected artist. Help Gabriel. Keep talking.*

"So, we've actually been seeing each other since last summer. We just wanted to keep it a secret. He's so famous and he knew I didn't want any media attention. Part of why he accepted the

Los Angeles contract was to be close to me." She paused and dug her fingernails into her thighs, the pain keeping her focused on pushing through the lies.

"We were planning on keeping it on the down low for a while longer, but now with the injury and the uncertainty of what will happen with his career…" She gazed down, unable to meet anyone's eyes.

"Keep what on the down low? For the love of god Dylan, tell us what." Sam piped in.

"We're engaged. Now that everything has changed, I want us to move into the other guesthouse while he recuperates and decides what to do next." Her fingernails were talons gouging her legs.

"Engaged?" Amanda's eyes widened.

"Move in here?" Her dad's brows had disappeared to his hairline.

"What the hell?" Her twin's eyes rounded into saucers, her expression almost comical.

She held up both hands again. Of course they were shocked. The only ones who even knew of Gabriel's existence were Amanda and Sam. And maybe Jake and Holt because her sisters probably told their guys everything.

"I'm sorry I kept it secret, but we just thought it was for the best." She shrugged and pasted what she hoped was a convincing smile on her face.

"You didn't trust your own family to tell us you've been involved with this guy for a *year*? And *engaged*? You've only been in the same country for weeks?" Her dad's telltale tic started in his jaw and his large hands gripped the sturdy oak table.

Uh-oh. Time to kick her performance to its crescendo.

"Dad, you more than anyone understand how much the paparazzi changed our lives." She stared at her father, willing the real emotion shone through. "I'm sorry that I was secretive and of course I trust everyone, but it wasn't all up to me. Gabriel has a lot of obligations as well. I didn't mean to hurt anyone."

"But engaged, Dylan? How much time have you actually spent with him?" Angela's voice was gentle, but her dark eyes reflected her concern.

"We haven't even met the guy." Holt added.

"Well, you'll meet him soon enough. He's got his second surgery today and then once he's discharged, he's got a long road ahead of him to recover." Telltale heat rose in her cheeks.

Her dad was shaking his head. "Dylan, this isn't like you. Engaged to someone none of us have met and how well can you know him? I mean–"

"Dad, just trust me on this, okay? I've almost told you guys several times but the timing was never right. Can you please be supportive and give him a chance?"

"You love him, honey? Like really love him for the long haul?" Angela's hand rested on her father's arm, her face creased with concern.

Tension shot through every nerve in her body– how in the world were they going to pull this off under her family's scrutiny? Dylan crossed her legs, her toes, and her fingers under the shelter of the large wood table. She nodded her head enthusiastically, unable to actually utter the words out loud. Love—the truth was they'd spent one passionate night together and essentially had three dates after that. If you counted a hospital visit and being propositioned by his mother to this ridiculous scheme as dates.

Why had she thought she could just tell her family they were engaged and they'd all be like, great! That's our romantic Dylan. Can't wait to meet him and plan the wedding. Sometimes she wished she'd been born with a little more of the analytical brain her older sister Amanda had or the tougher shell her twin wore. She didn't have the defenses and the ability to hide her feelings.

If Gabriel's father was anywhere as tough as he sounded, they couldn't have any cracks in their façade. Not that her family would purposefully let the cat out of the bag, but any accidental comments could ruin Gabriel's plan to help his sister and figure out his own happy ending. She squared her shoulders and forced a casual smile. She'd tap into her hereditary acting genes—they had to be in there somewhere.

"Dylan?" Sam's dark eyes gleamed with hurt.

How would she ever fool her twin sister, much less make it up to her? They never kept secrets from each other. Ever.

Dylan met her twin's brown eyes, identical to her own. "I'm sorry I've had to do it this way. I hope you'll understand and forgive me."

Sam stared for another moment and silently communicated that the discussion was far from finished.

Dylan sighed and addressed their father. "So, is it okay if we move into the guesthouse in the next few weeks? I promise you'll all have plenty of time to get to know Gabriel. He's amazing." And that last sentence was absolutely true. He was amazing.

It wasn't like Dylan was trying to harm her family. She was trying to help herself and help Gabriel. And although she wasn't ready to admit it aloud, perhaps over the six months of their "engagement," she and Gabriel might really fall in love.

"Well honey, we love you and if you feel this strongly about him to get married, then we'll welcome him. But he and I *will* be talking." Her dad's expression softened slightly.

Dylan's belly churned at the idea of her dad interrogating Gabriel. Before they moved into the guesthouse, they needed to learn a lot more about each other. Otherwise, they'd never convince her family they'd been in a yearlong relationship. Besides the limited time they'd spent together and what she'd read online, she didn't know him. Not in the intimate ways engaged couples did. Real engaged couples.

So that's what they'd be doing while he was recovering in L.A. Otherwise their cover would be blown to smithereens.

Dylan rose from her seat and pasted a cheerful

smile on her face. "I'm going to head up to Gabriel's now. He's got surgery scheduled for first thing in the morning and I want to be with him."

She hurried from the room and was halfway down the hall when Sam caught her.

"Wait up."

Drat. She stopped and waited for her twin. "I need to hop in the shower and get on the road so I don't run into rush hour traffic." *And I don't want to lie to you.*

Sam fell into step alongside her. "What's really going on? Engaged? You've barely even talked about this guy and suddenly you've been secretly in love for a year? Come on."

Dylan kept walking and answered without turning her head. She couldn't meet her sister's eyes. "Sam, you've been pre-occupied with your own life since I returned from Paris. You and Holt got married, breeding season's been hectic, and I just thought it was best to keep to myself. I'm sorry if I hurt your feelings. I really didn't mean to."

She dared a glance at Sam, whose full mouth was turned down at the corners. "Do you feel like I haven't been here for you? Have I neglected you? Oh Dylan, I'm so sorry."

A slice of remorse twisted in her heart. "No, no, no. I'm not trying to guilt trip you. I just think over the last year we've all done our own thing a little bit more, okay? And honestly, everything changed once Gabriel got to the States. I know it's fast, but everything with you and Holt happened quickly too." *Deflect.*

"You mean after we stopped wanting to rip each other's hair out?" Sam flashed her quick grin. "Okay, but this all still feels really sudden. You guys said you saw Holt and I falling for each other, but I really haven't heard or seen a thing with you. You've just seemed so focused on your painting."

"Well, I have been and it helped me when I was missing him. And I may have some good news on that front too. Look, I promise to share more. But I've got to hurry, okay?" She turned and pulled Sam into a hug.

Sam squeezed her back. "You better. I want to make sure you know I'm always here for you, okay?"

Dylan sighed. "Of course. I love you."

Dylan hurried to her bathroom and turned the shower on full-blast. Thank god that was over.

Time to get her butt in gear. If she and Gabriel had a shot at pulling off this hare-brained scheme, they had considerable work to do.

CHAPTER 11

GABRIEL BATTLED THE WALL OF heavy water confining him beneath the surface. No matter how strongly he thrashed his arms and legs, he couldn't seem to propel himself up and out of the depths. He shook his head again and tried to clear his vision. Why the hell was he confined like this? Almost like someone had chained him to boulders at the bottom of the ocean and he'd never escape.

"Mr. DuVernay, please try to relax. Please try to keep your arms by your sides." A high-pitched voice reached his ears.

With herculean effort, he managed to open his eyes. Blinding light assaulted him and he promptly shut them. Reality came flooding back. He was in the hospital. He'd awakened from surgery, so at least he wasn't dead and buried at sea. But if he would never run or play again, maybe his nightmare might be preferable to that unwelcome reality.

A few staff transferred him from the gurney to his hospital bed and he couldn't feel anything in his leg at all. Only numbness.

"Gabriel, how are you feeling?" Dylan's melodic husky voice asked.

He pried his eyes open again and there she was, like a titian angel by his side. His jaw relaxed. Last night, they'd hung out at his condo like it was any other night. His management team had assured him they'd handle the press and keep his privacy protected. If one more person told him not to worry and just focus on healing, he'd head butt them like he'd done one hundred and twenty times for goals on the field. Only Dylan's presence soothed the fury and anguish.

Funny because before he'd always been stimulated around her and overtaken by her sensuality and sparkling energy. Now her warmth, kindness, and understanding pacified him. But underlying nerves simmered beneath her sweet demeanor. He wasn't the only one whose life was changing forever.

"Gabriel?" She tilted her head, her eyes wide.

He shook his head. "Sorry. I'm okay. Any news?"

"No. The doctor said everything went well and he'd be in to explain." She offered an encouraging smile.

"Did he say when I can get out of here?" The parts of his body he could feel prickled with restless electric energy.

She shook her head and the corners of her plump red lips twitched. "Um, you just got back from surgery, so it will probably be at least another five minutes."

He smiled at her attempt to cheer him up.

His surgeon entered the room. "Oh good, you're awake. You ready to hear this?"

Gabriel ground his teeth and nodded.

"So, the surgery went better than we could have hoped. I'm very pleased. We want to start your rehab the day after tomorrow. You'll be able to go home tomorrow. We just want to watch you today and make sure there are no complications."

"What does that mean? Will I run again? Play football?" Every muscle in his body, well the ones that still had feeling, locked up.

The doctor's expression didn't change. "No. I'm not going to give you false hope. But with proper rehab you should be able to walk without a limp and in time be able to exercise more vigorously. With the depth and severity of your injuries, walking without a limp is nothing short of a miracle."

Bile rose in Gabriel's throat, the acid bitter and choking. Walking without a limp was now a damn miracle? Not in his world. He struggled not to yell, rip off all the tubes attached to his body, and sprint out of the room. Oh yeah, he wasn't running anywhere. Possibly ever again. His head slumped back against the pillows.

"Can you really predict all of that at this point? Isn't it possible to use stem cells and other treatments to aid the healing process? Get better results?" Dylan asked.

Dr. Odhiambo shook her head. "There are all types of protocols which will help, but there are limits. It's best not to have unrealistic expectations." She backed up and headed toward the door. "I'll check back in with you tomorrow, Gabriel."

She left and his Maman entered. "I understand the surgery was successful?" She strode to his bedside and gazed down at him, sympathy shining in her eyes.

He nodded, but didn't trust himself to speak without cursing or losing his shit.

Dylan spoke first. "Good morning, Michele. The doctor said the surgery went very well, but she was quite pessimistic about Gabriel's future as an athlete."

His mom reached out and stroked her hand down his cheek. "I'm sorry, my love. Time will tell. Do you feel up to discussing the engagement? I've got some news and we must move quickly."

He opened his eyes and nodded. Anything was better than contemplating his ruined career.

"And Dylan, this of course includes you." His mom paused and kissed each of Dylan's cheeks in the customary French greeting.

Michele fished a small square box out of her classic black Chanel purse and offered it to Gabriel.

Still groggy, he stared at it, not quite understanding why she'd given it to him. A surgery gift?

"Open it, Gabriel." His mother prompted.

He flicked the lid open and gaped at the contents. He looked up at his maman and then shifted his gaze to Dylan, who stared at the jewelry box, her lips parted.

"This was your grand-mère's engagement ring

and her mother's ring before her. It's been in the DuVernay family for more than a century. Your father gave it to me thirty-three years ago. It is yours to give to your future bride." His mom's silver eyes shone as she smiled down at him.

Future bride? His grandmother's ring? Gabriel's heartbeat accelerated and sweat broke out along his upper lip. Suddenly the reality of the situation slammed into him. Now he not only had to deal with losing his dream career, rehabbing his knee, but also convincing his father, the ultimate cynic, that he was so in love that he was getting married?

Hell, marriage had always seemed like something for the distant future, after he'd retired from football. With his lifestyle and career, even a serious relationship made zero sense. Dylan was a beautiful and intriguing woman and he'd looked forward to dating her, maybe even having her as a girlfriend, but *future bride*?

"Oh no, I couldn't accept your family heirloom. We can get another ring. That's for your real..." Dylan bit her lip and dropped her gaze to the floor.

His maman flicked her hand impatiently. "*Alors.* Don't be silly. This engagement is real and you must accept this ring, otherwise Gabriel's father and the rest of our family will suspect something is amiss. There is no other option."

Gabriel stared at the sparkling jewelry. He must be *complètement fou.* Crazy. And so was Dylan for agreeing to it. Was she so desperate to become a famous artist? Of course he could understand her ambition because he'd been driven his whole life to be the best at and be applauded for being the best soccer player in the world.

"Gabriel. Dylan. Listen to me. Focus on right now. This is our best plan and you two need to convince everyone it is real or nobody will buy it. I'll leave the room, but before you leave the hospital, Dylan should have your ring on her finger and your manager needs to make an announcement, comprends?" His mother's jaw was clenched and her gaze flinty as she looked between them.

"Oui." Gabriel nodded. Now he was struggling to regulate his breathing.

"Yes, I mean oui." Dylan nodded, her usually rosy cheeks pale.

"Okay. Remember what's at stake Gabriel. Your sister. Your father. Your future. I know this is difficult and your future may not look like what you had hoped, but you must be strong." She leaned down, kissed his cheek, and exited the room.

Dylan stood awkwardly by his bed and the silence in the room grew heavy, like the weight of water he'd been drowning beneath. Was he supposed to propose now? Just giving her the ring in the cold and sterile hospital room wasn't exactly a loving or romantic proposal.

Hell, he was still half drugged out. But he had no choice. On that his mother was correct.

He looked up at her and gestured for her to come closer to the edge of his bed.

Gabriel's pupils were dilated and his drawn

expression inscrutable. Had his surgery drugs even worn off yet? Dylan perched delicately on Gabriel's hospital bed, careful not to disturb the riot of tubes in his arms or touch his bandaged elevated leg.

Her heart knocked against her ribs and her legs trembled. Even though her brain knew this was a business arrangement, her body hadn't received the message and betrayed her now.

Nobody had inspired this depth of feeling in her until she met Gabriel. But their time together had been brief and she figured she was just looking back at it with rose-colored glasses.

Getting temporarily pretend engaged to him in his hospital room wasn't exactly dreamy.

If she'd ever envisioned getting engaged, she'd figured she'd be madly in love and it would be romantic and passionate and magical. In her girl-ish dreams, she'd always imagined love at first sight and being swept off her feet. She swallowed down the disappointment that she'd never have a true first engagement to the man she loved. That "first" was effectively off the table.

She couldn't lie to herself. Over the last year, both of her sisters had fallen madly in love and committed to their forever partners. She'd never seen either of them this happy or fulfilled. Although she'd felt the pressure to end her own single status when family and friends would slyly ask when it was her turn, she hadn't worried about it too much. One major benefit of the pre-tend engagement would be avoiding the curious stares and nosy questions from people now.

She'd given her word and she'd follow through. Her art came first and his mom's connections might be the big break she needed for connoisseurs to be exposed to her work. All she needed was the chance. That's all. So she'd compartmentalize the rest for now.

"Dylan." Gabriel reached out one long hand and clasped hers in a surprisingly strong grip.

She met his emerald gaze and exhaled an unsteady breath. "Gabriel."

"You're shaking. This is crazy, non?" He flashed his white teeth and squeezed her hand more firmly.

"Completely. Are we really going to be able to pull this off?" Tingles shot up her arm from where they were connected.

He stroked his thumb along her palm and she shivered. Before she could answer, he drew her hand to his lips and brushed his mouth along her skin. He met her gaze. "Our attraction to each other is not faked. I've never met anyone like you, Dylan."

Mesmerized by the heat in his expression, all she could do was nod.

"I am sorry we must do this here, but..." He shrugged a shoulder. "Pretend I am kneeling instead of in this bed."

He interwove his fingers with hers and tugged her closer. She caught herself with her other hand on the pillow next to his shiny chestnut hair. "Gabriel, be careful. I don't want to hurt you."

He chuckled. "I can't feel my leg and you are light as a feather."

Now she was practically lying across his lap with her hand on his firm chest. His heart pounded almost as fast as hers. Could the cocky charming Frenchman be nervous too? Heat pooled in her belly—yes she was turned on even when he was swathed in bandages and propped up by a hospital bed. "You're sure?"

He pulled her in a few inches closer and kissed her, his lips parting hers gently yet firmly. Helpless to resist him, she sighed and deepened the kiss. She shifted one hand into his hair and dug her fingers into the silky strands. Their tongues tangled and stroked and Dylan's bones melted.

He ended the kiss and now his customary wicked grin returned. "I might be injured, but I am not dead. I, for one, am liking the idea of sharing your bed every night."

Dylan shifted back, but didn't pull her hand from his. She licked her lips and his eyes hooded. "But you're just out of surgery, so you need to get better."

"Oh, I'm just fine above the knees." His grin deepened and he winked.

Resisting the urge to yank down the sheets and reveal his carved abs, Dylan sat back and crossed her legs. Like Gabriel said, they'd be sleeping together every night. She shivered again. "Gabriel. We're in the hospital."

"Fine." He pouted and then exhaled. "Dylan McNeill. You are an incredible, beautiful, talented woman. Will you do me the honor of becoming my fiancée and spending the rest of…" He sighed. "Will you become my fiancée for as long as makes sense for both of us to fulfill our dreams?"

Dylan's heart clenched. For a moment, she'd fallen into a trance with his accented raspy voice proposing to her. Until he got to those final words that emphasized this engagement wasn't real and was only a six-month business arrangement. That, unlike her sisters, she wasn't getting her own happily-ever-after. No words of love or forever. She swallowed down the sudden lump clogging her throat.

"Yes. I will be your fake fiancée for as long as we both shall need." She managed to speak clearly, although for some reason, hot tears burned behind her eyes. Ridiculous.

Gabriel winced and lowered his gaze. He released her hand, reached for the velvet box, and flipped it open. She swiped at her eyes to make sure he wouldn't notice her escalating emotions. No place for her to succumb to the strange ache behind her heart. When he looked up again and turned the box to her, her face was composed. She hoped.

She gasped when the overhead fluorescent lights shot brilliant sparks off the multifaceted ring. A Princess cut diamond flanked by two vibrant emeralds sat on a delicate pave band lined with shimmering diamonds. The enormous stone managed to look elegant and majestic, despite the size. Good grief, would the piece of jewelry weigh down her hand so much her hand would drag along the ground?

Gabriel took the ring out of the box and slid it on her ring finger. "It fits perfectly. Do you like it?" His looked up.

She pulled her gaze from the incredible ring and smiled at him. "Um, yes I like it. It's the most beautiful ring I've ever seen." Like it had been made especially for her. *Too bad it's temporary.*

"For the most beautiful woman I've ever seen."

Color rose in her cheeks. He was so smooth with his compliments and that accent killed her. "You tell that to all the girls."

He frowned and his voice grew brusque. "Non. No, I don't. From now on you are my only woman and we need to remember that. Now can you give me my phone from the drawer? I must call my manager, tell him I'm out of surgery, and have him draft the press release."

The heat cooled as quickly as it had risen. Back to business. "Of course." She handed him the phone. "I'll be back in a little while. I'm going to go get some coffee. Can I bring you anything?" She needed space. Now.

He shook his head, already with the phone up to his ear.

Game on.

CHAPTER 12

SHOWTIME. DYLAN SLAMMED THE TRUNK of her white Audi A4 closed. They'd stowed a few suitcases and boxes in it–apparently Gabriel traveled light. For the last week, she'd been driving back and forth while waiting for him to receive his doctor's release, secure the best rehab specialists in San Diego, and tie up what felt like a million loose ends.

At home, she was finishing up one more piece to show Gabriel's mother and discussing the best timing to connect with various galleries in New York and Europe. She'd also been running around like the energizer bunny putting together finishing touches on Jake and Amanda's engagement party. Somehow it had gone from an intimate gathering to a major bash, which wouldn't have been an issue prior to this whole situation with Gabriel.

"Are you ready?" She slipped on her seatbelt and turned toward her cranky passenger.

Gabriel's eyes popped open. "Oui." The seat was back as far as it would go to allow him to keep his left leg extended for the ninety-minute drive down to Pacific Vista Ranch.

Dylan navigated the winding streets of Manhattan Beach, avoiding the throngs of swim-suit-covered tourists streaming off of the sidewalks in their march toward the crystal blue ocean. Summer in Southern California only seemed to get busier and busier, especially in the charming popular beachside towns. The sun bestowed warmth from its position in the cornflower blue sky, the salty breeze wafted into the car's open windows, and chatter and laughter filled the air.

"Merci. You're probably happy not to have to drive up here anymore. I know it's, how do you call it, an ache in the butt?" He angled his gaze toward her.

Dylan laughed. "You mean a pain in the butt. It will be nice to get settled and start moving forward with everything. I know you're eager to start rehab with your Sports Medicine group."

He waved a hand. "Ache, pain—so many expressions to remember. You're right. The team down there is supposed to be the best and I'm ready."

She nodded. "So, should we do some more quizzing before you meet my family?"

"Oui. Okay, your favorite color is green. Or did you just say that because you love my eyes?" He batted his dark lashes.

Heat flooded her cheeks. Busted. "You're so modest. I love green and, yes, your eyes just happen to be absolutely gorgeous. Like you didn't know that already. Your favorite color is blue and we know that's not because of my eyes. Your birthday is December 18ᵗʰ, Sagittarius and turning 32 this year, right?" *No way would she admit she knew his birthday was the same day as Brad Pitt's or that she thought he was just as hot as the movie star.*

"You've got the most beautiful eyes I've seen. Like sweet molten chocolate—my favorite treat." His grin grew mischievous. "Your birthday is July 22ⁿᵈ, the cusp between Leo the Lion and Cancer, and you'll be 29 next month. Your sister was born three minutes after you and she is more of the fierce lion and you are more of the sensitive crab, non?"

"We've got this down. The toughest person to fool will be Sam. As twins, we've got a kind of sixth sense about each other. She's already suspicious. Luckily, she knows I can be secretive and I did tell her about our night last summer." She paused and willed the blush in her cheeks to subside. "I think it makes sense if we don't know everything about our childhoods and all that because we have been long distance, right?"

"Maybe. But we talked a lot, right? And didn't we write long flowery love letters?" His brows knit together. "Am I meeting everyone at once? Or how will this work when we arrive?"

Dylan's heart kicked at the suggestion of love letters from Gabriel. If only. She pulled onto the 405 Freeway heading south toward San Diego. She closed the windows and flipped on the air conditioning.

Once she'd settled into a middle lane amongst all the speeding cars whizzing by them, she replied.

"Well, it's possible my stepmom, Angela, or Sam might come over to the cottage when we get there. But most likely it will be at dinner tonight."

"We won't be having family dinners every night, will we?" Gabriel drew back, his eyes wide.

She shook her head. "Don't sound so excited. We could if we wanted to and Angela's an amazing cook. But we've got a full kitchen in our guesthouse. We have family dinners on Sunday nights and during the week, if I feel like going up I just let Angela know. I'm not much of a cook, are you?"

"Oui, I am a good cook because I got tired of eating or ordering out. I'm just not used to a big, close family. I left home early for my career and am used to being on the road. If you think sharing meals with your family will help convince them this engagement is real, I can play the doting fiancé."

Dylan's gut clenched. Of course he could play the doting fiancé. Charm was his middle name and he was very smooth. Very French. Although she knew he didn't mean anything by it, every time she was reminded that this arrangement was a business one, her stomach hurt. Life would have been much easier if they were sharing a simple relationship while she focused on her art. Now, there were so many more layers to it all.

Sure, his mother was compiling an impressive list of introductions for her and Dylan needed to keep that her primary focus. But the added pressure of having to pretend she and Gabriel were truly in love and were planning on getting married was overwhelming.

Before she'd been secure in their mutual attraction, but now who knew?

She was helping him and his sister achieve their goals. He was helping her. Would this business aspect to the relationship render their real feelings meaningless?

"Dylan? Did I say something wrong? I didn't mean to offend you." He laid one bronzed long fingered hand on her arm.

Like every single time he touched her, sparks shot up her arm. "No, sorry. It's time to learn all the mundane things about each other. Favorite color. Fondest memories. Favorite wine. Books and movies and religion and politics. In that order." She really needed to move off the personal information and be objective. Ha, not exactly her modus operandi.

He tilted his head and then replied. "Okay, I like thrillers and some mysteries if they're dark and twisty. I like non-fiction and history and philosophy. Movies I like thrillers too and all the old-fashioned movies from my country. You know, with Isabelle Adjani and Gerard Depardieu."

She nodded. "Thrillers and mysteries. Philosophy? That surprises me a little bit."

He scowled. "Why? Because I'm a professional athlete?"

Her mouth dropped. "Oh no, I didn't mean it that way. Again, this is why we need to discuss this stuff before we see my family. Who do you like? DesCartes? Simone de Beauvoir? Voltaire? All French or any Americans or Brits?"

"Oui, also Camus and Sartre. I enjoy Thoreau as well."

Dylan smiled. "We have similar tastes. Well, what about artists and how much do you know about my art and influences?"

"See, this will be easy to remember. Perhaps one night we will discuss over some nice Cabernet. You told me the Impressionists have influenced you and you've built your style from that base. Impressionist is my favorite. I'm open to many styles and saw a lot growing up with my mother's obsession with it. I am not a fan of many modern styles, though. You know, the red dot on canvas or some other such silliness."

"Definitely. And I'll show you my paintings in the next few days. Good to know your mother trained you well. It will also make sense that we have a love of art in common."

"Did none of your other men have an interest in art?" Gabriel's voice deepened.

Dylan frowned. "Some, but the few longer-term relationships I had the guys didn't."

"Have you been in love? Close to marriage before?" Gabriel rasped.

Dylan sighed. No avoiding the personal stuff. "I thought I was in love when I was younger. Dated one man for a few years. We were too young and it just fizzled out because my art always came first. So no."

"I cannot believe it. You're so beautiful and special. Are these American men idiots?" His strong brow furrowed.

"Gabriel, I don't want to get into it, okay? You haven't either, right?" No need to delve into the myriad of reasons Dylan preferred keeping her relationships short and not too intimate. Gabriel didn't need to know about her abandonment issues, not when their relationship was truly pretend.

"Non. Like you, my career has always come first and we stay very busy through the season and pre-season. And with how much I travel." He paused and hissed out a breath. "Traveled. How much I traveled. It made it too hard. I always figured I had plenty of time." He turned and looked out the window, his jaw granite hard.

Dylan drove in silence for a few minutes. What could she say? His life had been completely up-ended. But they both needed to focus on the present and ensure their scheme worked. Plenty of time to allow her emotions free rein later.

"I'm sorry. Well, we have that in common. Career first. Lots of relationships, just no time to settle down. We both love Monet, Manet, and Degas. I do *not* like thriller movies and I haven't seen many French films. You'll have to show me a few."

"Mais oui. But one more personal question. Have you ever had your heart broken?" He turned to look at her, his expression solemn.

She felt the heat of his gaze searing her cheek.

"By a man?"

"Or any way?" His voice lowered.

She gripped the steering wheel. "Not the way you think. My heart has never been the same since my mom died the way she did. That accident changed our lives forever and losing her..." A lump lodged in her throat. Damn it, she wasn't going to cry now.

"I'm sorry, Dylan. I don't mean to stir up the past. You've already told me how the nastiness of the paparazzi forced your family to start over at the ranch. I understand how cutthroat they can be and I'm sorry it hurt you." He brushed his strong hand along her thigh and heat shot straight to her center.

"You've had to deal with them too. Do you think they'll be aggressive with you?" She exhaled slowly.

He shrugged. "I don't know. But they only focused on my performance and the women I'd be seen with. Whatever stories they fabricated about me didn't matter as long as it didn't embarrass my family, who knew to ignore the outlandish ones. I didn't have to handle what you have."

"I'm sure they'll be interested where you disappeared to though." Dylan's fingers gripped the leather-bound steering wheel tight.

"Don't worry. My publicist is good. All they need to know for now is that I'm recuperating with the help of my lovely fiancée. You said your ranch is very private, with security, non?"

"Yes. Especially after what happened with the

movie last summer. But later we realized the story is old and there's no reason for them to revive it again. I just hope your groupies don't bother us." Her gut tightened.

He laughed. "Groupies? Non. If I'm not playing matches, they've got no reason to be seen with me. They'll go for the best players. That's over." Abruptly his laughter stopped and he turned and stared out the window again.

Her heart ached for his fresh pain. "I'm sorry. Let's keep going. We're only forty-five minutes away. Religion? Politics?"

He sighed. "The easy topics, no? We were raised Catholic. My family still attends mass at the small church near our estate, but nobody is a zealot. Politics? I try to avoid that topic at all costs. But I guess you'd call me a moderate."

"We're Catholic too, but I confess none of us really go to church. We did when we were little girls, but it kind of fell off. I prefer to think of a higher power as simply being kind and following the golden rule, you know? And I'm moderate to liberal. We don't debate politics a lot at home, despite how crazy the world is right now. At least not at the dinner table."

"So are we getting married in the church then?" Gabriel asked.

Dylan's foot slammed on the brake, jerking them out of the seventy-mile-per-hour pace. "What?"

He shrugged one shoulder. "Well, won't your parents and sisters ask if we've thought about where we will marry?"

Dylan's heartbeat accelerated. "God, I hadn't thought that far ahead. Sam and Holt married on the ranch and Amanda and Jake will too. I don't want to get ahead of ourselves."

"But what will we say?" He persisted.

Dylan grimaced. "That this has all happened really fast and we're focusing on being engaged, spending time together in the same country, and you healing."

"Huh." He grunted.

"Gabriel, this is all sudden, not just for you and me, but for my family. I think it would be strange if we already had a wedding date and cake flavors picked out." Had he forgotten this was make-believe? Not helpful to her myriad of emotions.

"I suppose. You don't think they'll believe I'm trying to get my green card, do you?"

Dylan laugh snorted and shook her head. "It never occurred to me so I doubt it will for them. When does your visa expire?"

"Well, with the team, I had no issues. If I am fully released, there may be problems. My lawyers told me to focus on rehab and they'd handle it." His gravelly voice deepened.

"Okay, that's good." *Drat.* Just what they needed–an immigration issue on top of the now really complicated bed they were making.

Dylan turned onto the familiar winding road leading to Pacific Vista Ranch and sighed out a relieved breath. Part of her was eager to get out of the car because the intimacy of the conversation was becoming stifling. What had seemed like a viable solution now felt like the height of lunacy.

Because her feelings for Gabriel were anything but casual.

CHAPTER 13

DYLAN RAPPED ON THE DOOR of the guesthouse's ensuite master bathroom. Gabriel had been in the shower for what felt like forever. Although it was a three-minute walk to the main house along the scenic tree-shrouded path, the gravel and uneven terrain would be torture for Gabriel on crutches. If they were going to be on time for dinner, she needed to drive them—now.

"Oui?" His gravelly voice purred from the other side of the door.

"You almost ready? Dinner is at 6 and we don't want to be late. Can I do anything for you?" Because arriving late wouldn't be an auspicious start to their opening night performance.

The door whipped open and Dylan could only stare. Beads of moisture from the shower clung to his bronzed skin and contrasted beautifully with the white towel slung low around his narrow hips. Every single sculpted, lean muscle from his square pecs down his washboard abs to those carved V-shaped grooves that disappeared beneath the terry cloth beckoned to be stroked. Steam floated around him.

He quirked a brow, his smile wicked. "Oh, I could think of a few things we could do for each other, ma chérie." Tingles shot along her spine when his hot green gaze seared down her body.

Her mind blanked. Dinner, oh yeah, dinner with her family. "We really do need to get up to the house and you're injured."

"Just my knee. Everything else is fine. Come here." He stretched one sleekly muscled arm toward her.

Unable to resist, she stepped forward, eliminating the space separating them. She inhaled his clean scent and every nerve ending in her body leapt at his proximity.

His arms snaked around her and drew her in the remaining inches to his half-naked body. She wound her arms around his strong neck, her lips parting in surrender. Eager. Passionate. His hands slid up into her hair, tugged her head back, and captured her mouth. She moaned and melted into the fiery kiss.

He growled low in his throat and pivoted without breaking their connection. The cool stone of the bathroom vanity pressed into her back. Her breasts smashed against his bare chest and his rigid length burned into her. Cradling her head with one hand, his other hand slid down to cup her breast and his fingers stroked and pinched her taut nipple.

"So good." She moaned against his lips and arched her back, needing more. Craving more. Her skin flamed and heat flooded her veins.

Lifting his head, he looked down, his emerald gaze hooded and his jaw carved from granite.

"Let me please you." He stroked his talented hands from her breasts down her waist and captured her hips, his caresses leaving streaks of fire along her body.

"Gabriel, your leg." She shivered and her breath caught when he lowered his head to nibble along the sensitive skin of her neck. He ignored her and lowered his head and bit her nipple lightly through the t-shirt and paper-thin bra she wore. Heat shot straight down and pooled low in her belly. She gripped his muscular arms, and her head dropped back. He reached one hand down between them and cupped her, stroking through her jeans.

She shuddered at the intense contact. "Gabriel, I..." *I want you inside me right now.*

"Ouch." He grunted and released her, grabbing onto the marble counter behind her.

His cry acted like a pail of icy water, extinguishing their shared passion. "Oh no, is your knee okay?" Had she kicked or hit him?

He leaned his forehead against hers, the weight of his powerful physique heavy against her. "It's okay. But we need a bed. This won't work." He gritted out the words.

"No Gabriel, we have to go up to dinner. We can't go to bed." She struggled, concentrating on not moving too quickly or jolting his leg again. Good lord, she felt like she could have climaxed right here with him, fully clothed.

Well, at least *she* was fully clothed.

He didn't budge. "Promise me. Later."

She shivered. Why not? Although she'd be playing a dangerous game with her heart, she could handle it, right? Why wouldn't they take advantage of living together? They'd probably fool her family a lot easier if they were intimate. Lord knows they'd be flushed and relaxed–an easily observed physical connection.

She reached up and clasped his head between her hands and kissed his sculpted mouth. "Yes. Later. But now you need to get dressed."

He pouted for a moment. "How long is dinner?"

She laughed at his expression. "Not too long. Do you need help getting dressed or will that make us even more late?" Perhaps this mock engagement situation wouldn't be so tough to fake, as long as she kept her heart protected and enjoyed herself with him. The benefits of having his sexy body all to herself for months was enticing.

He laughed and shifted away from her, picking up the crutches from where they were propped against the pale aqua walls. "I should be okay. You're too beautiful and tempting and your family might not appreciate how late we will be if I can lure you onto our bed."

She stepped aside so he could hobble into the room and get dressed. She plopped down on the garnet-colored velvet chaise lounge, a safe distance from the California King bed they would share tonight for the first time. Although there were two more bedrooms in the guesthouse, with

Dylan's luck, one of her sisters would barge in on them and discover them sleeping separately...the game would be up before it began. And again, sleeping with him wouldn't be a hardship.

As long as she could keep her emotions separate from their arrangement. Friends with benefits. She chanted the refrain silently in her mind. Friends with benefits. Or was it business partners with benefits?

When he was ready, she drove them up to the house. Nerves thrummed along her skin. Would she be able to convince the people who she loved the most and who knew her better than anyone that she was in love with Gabriel?

She ground her back teeth together—yes she absolutely could. Her twin might have the reputation as the stubborn sister, but Dylan could be just as stubborn if the occasion warranted.

When Gabriel shoved himself out of the car's passenger seat, pain pulsated from his knee to essentially every single cell in his body. He cursed under his breath—he was a DuVernay and he'd be damned if he got hooked on pain pills like some other injured athletes he knew. He'd already quartered his doctor's recommended dosage of heavy narcotics. But damn, experiencing every twinge, stab, and burn of pain was no joke.

Dylan's fragrant auburn hair brushed against him when she handed him his crutches. He fought not to yank her beautiful responsive body into him again. He might be stuck out on some horse ranch, but sleeping with her every night would make this whole situation a hell of a lot better.

"Let's do this." Dylan's cherry red lips split into an encouraging smile.

Something tightened in his chest. This woman's compassion and generosity blew him away. Now she was saving his ass and providing him a second chance to choose the life he wanted. Would she be receiving even half the benefits of their bargain with just introductions to galleries and no guarantees her work would be chosen? Dylan McNeill tugged at him in a way he'd never experienced. He resolved to be his best around her, no matter how bleak he felt about losing his career.

"Apres toi, ma belle." *After you, my beauty.*

He gazed up in appreciation at the sprawling cream-colored home, which boasted a terracotta tiled roof, expansive windows, and an explosion of brilliant green trees and multi-colored flowers. Before he'd crutched forward two paces, the massive wooden front door opened and a woman who could only be Dylan's twin rushed forward and hugged her.

"You made it." Her large dark eyes, so like his fiancée's, held a trace of warning.

"We did. Sam, this is Gabriel. Gabriel, this is my sister." Dylan's said.

Sam approached and he leaned in and kissed each cheek in the customary French greeting. "Enchantée. I cannot believe there are two of you. Your sister has told me all about you."

"Really?" Sam crossed her arms and stared at him. "Well, we haven't heard quite as much about you. Get ready for the cross-examination. Heads up—our dad is what you'd call overprotective."

Dylan frowned. "Crap. He better be nice."

Sam shrugged. "I'm sure it will be fine. But how the hell you two kept this a secret over the last year with how frequently Gabe is splashed all over the news is a mystery."

Screw this. "It's Gabriel, please. I'd think after what your family has experienced, you'd be less inclined to believe everything you see in the media."

Dylan spun to look at him, her gaze glowing with approval. She'd warned him her twin could be tough, but nobody could match what he'd had to handle with his own father, so he wasn't worried about the McNeills. And if all else failed, he could act like he didn't understand. People were always willing to believe he wasn't fluent in English.

Sam grinned. "That's the spirit, Gabriel. I figured the man who could handle my sister and was also one of the most talented athletes in the world had to have some spine."

He stiffened.

Was one of the most talented athletes.

He forced his lips to curve up. Time to compartmentalize. For the next few hours he would be the charming fiancé and convince the McNeills he was the perfect husband for Dylan. Once again, the unfamiliar tightening in his chest hit him. Marriage had always seemed like something light years away. But now he was confident he could convince anyone he couldn't wait to marry Dylan.

When they entered the house, Gabriel paused to admire the soaring ceilings, wide hallways, and pale cream walls. He loved the architecture in Southern California and the Spanish-style architecture of their estate contrasted starkly with his family's eighteenth century home/chateau. Although they'd maintained and updated it, it lacked this sense of newness he loved so much in America.

The crutches prohibited the opportunity to check out the glimpses of large rooms through wide open doors as they progressed toward what he assumed was the dining room. Voices carried down the hallway and grew louder as they approached. He hissed out an exhale and squared his shoulders. Well, as much as he could square them with these damned crutches digging into his underarms.

"The happy couple has arrived." Sam announced and preceded them into the expansive room.

Fragrant aromas filled the air and his stomach growled when he inhaled the mouthwatering spicy scents. Gabriel surveyed the large open kitchen. Several people gathered around an enormous long oak dining table set with colorful yellow dishes and laden with platters of food.

A tall strong-featured sandy haired man approached him. "Welcome to our home, Gabriel,

I'm Chris McNeill." His smile was tight and his eyes were guarded.

Uh-oh.

An attractive brunette stepped up and laid her hand on Mr. McNeill's arm. Her warm smile was welcoming. "Gabriel, we're thrilled to meet you. I'm Angela, Dylan's stepmom. I hope you're hungry because I made my enchiladas."

He returned her smile. "Thank you so much for welcoming me into your home. I apologize for not coming sooner, but my schedule…"

"Don't apologize. They understand." Dylan brushed her arm along his shoulder. "Let's sit down so you don't have to deal with these crutches for a while."

A couple of guys, one of them huge and dark and another lean and blond, sipped on beers and watched and waited. A slender blonde woman with an enigmatic expression, radiated protectiveness from across the room. She must be Amanda, Dylan's older sister.

A pang of regret filled him at his lackadaisical attitude back when the paparazzi snapped photos of him with so many women. He had his work cut out for him to convince Dylan's family he was in love and ready to settle down.

"I've put you on the end so you can keep your leg elevated on that little ottoman." Angela smiled at him and pulled out the chair at the head of the table. "Everyone else, have a seat."

"You're too kind. Merci." Whew, this way at least Chris McNeill was all the way at the far end of the table. Something told him the patriarch would be the toughest sell.

Dylan sat on his left and rested her hand on his arm.

"Hey Gabe, I'm Holt. Welcome to the family." Holt gave a crooked grin and saluted him with his longneck beer. Seemed genuine and a hint of sympathy flashed across the guy's movie star face.

"Gabriel." Damn it, he couldn't help himself, but no way was he going with this shortened version of his name. He loved America, but his name was Gabriel.

"Gabriel, I'm Amanda and this is my fiancé, Jake." Dylan's elder sister's voice was cool, but not cold. Her fiancé looked like the actor who was married to the Colombian sitcom actress. This family looked more Hollywood than horse ranch to him.

"Nice to meet you both." He returned her smile and returned Jake's nod. Those two were the quiet ones in the family. But that didn't mean winning them over would be simple.

"What can I get you to drink Gabriel? Dylan?" Angela asked.

"Beer would be great, thank you." He reached out and clasped Dylan's hand on the table. Her strong slender fingers laced with his and heat sparked up his arm. Immediately, his body stiffened in his now seemingly automatic reaction to her, just as it had in the bathroom. Only an hour or two until they could return to their cozy cottage.

"You know I always love a beer with your enchiladas. I hope you like spicy." Dylan grinned at Gabriel.

Once they had their drinks, the food was passed around the table. Gabriel's mouth watered as he loaded up his plate with enchiladas, dished out some black beans, and crisp green salad. For a few moments everyone ate in silence. Gabriel savored every delicious bite.

Maybe tonight her parents would go easy on them.

"So, Gabriel, tell us how you two managed to keep your relationship under wraps for so long?" Chris asked from the end of the table.

Or not.

Gabriel set down his fork and glanced at Dylan. A small line formed between her dark arched brows. He reached for her hand under the table and squeezed.

"Good question." He smiled at everyone around the table. "Well, both Dylan and I value discretion and chose to keep everything private. She shared what happened last summer and we didn't want any more attention on your family or mine."

Dylan piped in. "We weren't sure if Gabriel would get the L.A. contract, so it didn't make sense to tell everyone beforehand."

Chris frowned. "I understand keeping it private to the outside world. But with family? Dylan, it feels like you couldn't trust us."

Amanda added with a shake of her head, "Exactly." She looked at Gabriel, her gaze searching. "I mean, both Sam and I got engaged and you didn't mention you were seeing anyone?"

Gabriel swallowed. Apparently Dylan was close to her sisters like he was close to his. Maybe they could fool the parents, but the siblings weren't going to be an easy sell. Time to notch it up.

"I–" Dylan began.

Gabriel held up a hand. "This is all my fault. Dylan wanted to tell you, but I wasn't comfortable. My manager and I had been working to get control of my public image, especially with the move to the U.S. We wanted as much of the focus to be on my work on the field and less about my private life. Your family is high profile. My family is high profile. It would have been distracting."

"So your family knew and we didn't?" Sam demanded.

He shook his head. "Non. We've kept it from them too. We're telling you first. Please forgive Dylan–I shouldn't have put her in this type of position." *Wasn't that an understatement? Damn.*

"Look, you guys. Does it really matter? What's the big deal? Can't you just be happy for us?" Dylan's voice rose and when he glanced at her, her eyes shone with unshed tears and two flags of color were stamped across her cheeks.

"Oh sweetie, we're happy for you. It's just a lot out of the blue, you know?" Amanda smiled at her younger sister.

Sam sat back against her seat with a huff, crossed her arms, and glared at him. "We don't keep secrets in this family. If you're joining us, you better learn that now."

He rubbed his hand along Dylan's slender back, trying not to react to the silky velvet skin along her bare shoulders. She was trembling. Damn it, she was really upset.

"I'm sorry. You're right. I'm happy to be here now, even under the circumstances. We love each other very much."

"But would we know about this if you hadn't been injured? Or if you hadn't gotten the L.A. deal? Would Dylan suddenly be moving to Europe?" Sam demanded.

"Sam." Angela scolded from the other end of the table.

"What?" She shrugged. "I'm really sorry Gabriel, but I'm just having a tough time figuring out how my twin sister kept something like this from me."

"Sam." Dylan's voice was tight. "You and I can talk later. I had my reasons and I appreciate all of you just accepting this and moving on. Unless you want us to go back to L.A.?"

Gabriel jolted. Go back to L.A.? Would she really move for him? It would be a hell of a lot easier to live in his condo in Manhattan Beach just the two of them, instead of being with her whole family.

"Of course not. We want you here." *Where we can keep an eye on you*, Mr. McNeill silently admonished.

Silence fell over the table for a few awkward seconds. Gabriel's knee throbbed and his palms were damp.

"Can you pass the beans?" Jake spoke for the first time.

Like magic, the tension evaporated and everyone started talking at once and focusing more on the meal. Gabriel exhaled.

"It will be fine. Sorry they're so over-protective." Dylan whispered and tightened her grasp on his hand.

He shrugged. "Having a family who cares is a good thing." His own father would probably be much worse.

With a gentle tug, he pulled her in and pressed his lips to her full soft ones. Heat scorched through his veins. He'd eat fast and plead pain in his knee, which hurt like a bitch, and hurry back to the guesthouse with her. Otherwise, he'd implode.

The McNeills' dinner table became a lively sharing of stories punctuated with barks of laughter. Obviously, Chris and Angela were deeply in love with each other and with their children. Sam gestured wildly with her hands and commanded the table's attention when she spoke—she could be an honorary Frenchwoman. Despite having an identical face to Dylan's, Sam's mannerisms revealed her unique personality.

Holt and Jake seemed to fit in. Jake the brawny firefighter was obviously more of the strong, silent guy and Holt the retired stuntman was also a talker like his wife. Where did Gabriel fit in with the McNeills?

Truth be told, he wasn't sure he did. If he and

Dylan weren't trying to fool them, he'd be completely relaxed. Even so, he felt comfortable in this loud, homey atmosphere, so different from the formal environment his father favored. Maybe a close-knit clan wasn't a fantasy after all. Dylan was lucky to have this kind of home life.

Although he was glad family dinners weren't a nightly affair. His shoulder blades twitched at the thought of spending too much time under the McNeills' scrutiny. No, he'd lived independently and on his own terms for too long.

Time to head back to the guesthouse and seduce his fiancée.

CHAPTER 14

DYLAN HELD THE DOOR OPEN for Gabriel and he crutched his way into the main living space of their home. Their home. Even the fact they were living together was surreal. He smiled his crooked grin at her and every nerve in her body jumped to attention. Those brilliant green eyes, chiseled cheeks, and sculpted jawline made up one of the most intriguing faces she'd ever seen. The slight bump on his nose saved him from perfection. His face wasn't just classically handsome, it was compelling.

Just as she wanted to jump his bones and break this crazy sexual tension between them, her fingers itched to paint him. Would he let her?

"Do you want something to drink or to watch a movie or something?" Was it rude of her to just want to shortcut to the bedroom and finish what they'd started before dinner?

He shook his head and continued down the hallway to the master bedroom. "Let's skip that. Join me."

She smiled and hurried to catch up with him. They turned together into the spacious bedroom, dominated by the gigantic California King and she froze. Suddenly reality crashed down on her–this wasn't simply a fun fling or friends with benefits. Now they were forever linked because when the pretend relationship ended, they would have to engineer a break-up. They could never admit the engagement had been fake. She scowled.

"Why the frown, chérie?" Gabriel had reached the bed and reclined back, propping the crutches against the nightstand.

His t-shirt stretched across his leanly muscled chest and broad shoulders, distracting her. She swallowed, her throat suddenly dry. "Nothing. Just hate seeing you hurting like this." *A half truth was better than nothing.*

"I know what would make me feel a lot better." His eyes hooded and he patted the bed beside him.

The few steps to reach him felt more like a long trek under his unwavering gaze and sexy smile. She perched on the edge of the bed, on his uninjured side.

He wrapped one sinewy arm around her, and drew her down to join him. Even with their clothes on, the heat from his bronzed skin flamed through her. He slid his fingers into her hair and tugged her closer. Goosebumps erupted along her skin.

"Cold?" He rasped in that sexy as hell accent.

She shook her head. Tease–no way he could miss that her skin was on fire. Her gaze remained locked with his until he closed the space between them and brushed his lips against hers.

Her mouth parted and she sighed into the kiss, savoring the tender tangling of their tongues and his tart taste. Without warning, he deepened the kiss and gentleness transformed to urgency. Passionate urgency. When his powerful hands clasped her hips, lifting her on top of him in one swift motion, her nipples pebbled and her insides grew molten.

When her core pressed directly into his impressive erection, she moaned and her head fell back. She rocked her hips against his rigid length, savoring the feel of him beneath her. She shifted forward and stroked her fingernails lightly down his chest and smiled when his small flat nipples hardened beneath his thin cotton shirt. Without breaking his gaze, she grabbed the hem and shoved it up.

He pulled off his t-shirt, and she sighed with pleasure looking down at the tempting man beneath her. She stroked her hands down his sculpted chest, trailed her fingernails across his carved abs, and stopped to tug the drawstring on his board shorts.

She tightened the grip of her thighs, careful to avoid his injured leg. "Are you sure I won't hurt you?"

He laughed softly and covered her hands with his. "Be gentle with me."

He reached for her, but she shook her head and he crossed his muscular arms behind his head, his eyes hot. A surge of pure feminine power rushed through her veins. He was *hers,* and she wanted to take control. And him watching her only made her hotter.

"Dylan—" He growled when she ground her hips against him again.

"Shh…let me make you feel better." She leaned down and trailed open-mouthed kisses along his tanned skin, inhaling his delicious masculine scent.

She took her time and tasted, caressed, and kissed until she reached his waistband. Gently peeled it open to reveal his bronzed skin before she lowered her head and slid her mouth over him. Taut muscles twitched and jumped beneath her attention, his body like velvet covered steel. His hips jerked and he fisted his hands in her hair. His breathing grew harsh and he muttered her name. His arousal only spurred her on, sending liquid heat directly to her center.

She lifted her gaze and ran her tongue along her top lip. "I want more." She started to lower her head again, the thrill of bringing him pleasure spurring her on.

He growled low in his throat. "No more. Come here. Now." Drew her up along his strong physique, somehow managing to tug off her t-shirt and bra. His skills weren't limited to the soccer field.

She peeled off her long, gauzy skirt and lacy thong, applauding herself for wearing something with an elastic band. The moment her bare skin met his, she melted into him. He pulled her face down to meet his, crushing his lips against hers. His hands were everywhere, stroking down her back, cupping her ass, and all the while she was crushed against his rock-hard erection. She wiggled against him. She wanted him now.

"Gabriel, please, I want you inside me."   She was ready.

"I need to taste you first." He gripped her hips, lifted her, and positioned right above his mouth.

Who was she to refuse him? She was a trembling sweaty mess of nerves, but she braced her hands on the wall behind his head. Slowly, oh so slowly, he lowered her to meet his eager mouth. He stroked her with his talented tongue and lightly began nibbling and teasing. Desire surged through her, fast and hot. If he hadn't been holding her so tightly, she would have flown off the bed.

She began to move, seeking, welcoming, seizing every ounce of pleasure he offered. His hands were everywhere now and he thrust one blunt finger inside her, than two. Tremors started pulsing through her and she cried out and rocked against him. She collapsed on top of him, her entire body ablaze.

Heaven. She'd died and gone to heaven.

"Dylan, babe." He rasped against the skin of her hip.

She jolted. Oh no, she was probably suffocating him. He helped her slide back down his body until her mouth met his. Tasting herself on his lips stoked her desire. His cock pushed against her and she pulled away from him for a moment to grab a condom out of the nightstand drawer.

She positioned herself above him and the anticipation mounted. Leaning back, she helped him roll on the protection, eager to feel him inside her again after so many months.

"You ready for me?" She teased, loving the intense focus on his face.

"Now." He reached up and intertwined his fingers with hers, never breaking their gaze. She reached down and grasped his solid length in her hand and slowly, inch by beautiful inch, sank down on him until he filled her completely.

She moaned and threw her head back, taking a moment to adjust to him inside her. His eyelids floated shut and he gripped her hips.

She began to move, sliding up a few inches and lowering back down. He groaned but allowed her to set the deliberate pace. Fire coursed through her veins and she leaned forward until her breasts pressed into his hot slick skin. His hands tightened on her hips, urging her on with whispered demands. She rode him until the bursts of pleasure gathered into an earth-shattering climax. He cried her name and followed her over the edge.

To the outside world, their relationship might be pretend, but in their intimate cocoon, everything was real.

CHAPTER 15

FIFTEEN MINUTES INTO A FRUITFUL yet stressful video call with Michele Gaillard DuVernay and Dylan was holding her own. Michele was actually sweet underneath her polished exterior. They'd shared a fascinating conversation about art, the latest trends, and how Dylan's niche could play into some upcoming exhibitions in Paris and Nice.

Dylan carried the laptop over to where several of her favorite paintings leaned against her studio's wall. She swallowed the tension flowing through her. Not only did Gabriel's mother want to see her work, she also wanted to see her studio.

Dylan squared her shoulders and angled the computer so Michele could see and began to narrate. "Okay, I'm showing you these organized by some different projects. This first group is the one I've proposed to a gallery in Laguna Beach. It's a study of sunset and sunrise from one of the ocean view pastures."

After a few long moments, Michele said, "Your use of light is remarkable and I love how they're all *en plein air*, outdoors. Your family's ranch is beautiful. And the rest?"

As she began to share her paintings, her nerves fell away and she explained her motivations behind each canvas. "Oui. Many of them are painted on the ranch. It's huge. Both my sisters are passionate about their work with the horses. These three are of Sam working with Hercules, our stallion."

Michele gave a low whistle. "Mon Dieu, what a magnificent animal. And your sister is stunning like you, you've captured the fire in her hair and her strength despite the size of the stud."

She continued along the wall, where she'd pulled out a few she'd painted on one of the rare occasions they'd gotten measurable rain. "I painted these a few winters ago. We'd been in a drought for seven years and usually don't get much rain. Everything was so pure and clean afterwards and more green than I'd ever seen it." *Almost as green as your son's eyes.*

"I'll definitely be able to get you showings at all the galleries that carry impressionist and romantic paintings. You do understand the galleries that have cutting edge and modern styles will not be open to you."

"Of course. That's never been my style and I don't foresee it. I do hope you can see my personal takes on the more classic styles." She held in a breath.

"Oui, in fact your work reminds me a little bit of Georgia Noble. Do you know her?"

Dylan's exhale flowed out and she nodded. "Yes, she's incredible. That's a great compliment, merci. Not too similar though?"

"Non, I don't think so. There's room for both of you, but the comparison will make it easier for me to describe your work." Michele's silvery gaze narrowed. "Any paintings not on your ranch?"

"I do have some scenes from other locations in California and also Paris and Reims." *And a whole collection dedicated to your son's gorgeous face, but those won't see the light of day.*

"Parisian paintings and champagne country? Those might be perfect for some of the galleries here in France. Dylan, I must confess I am thrilled to see you possess true talent. Of course I would have still made the introductions because it's our bargain, but now I feel confident your work will speak for itself." Gabriel's mother's voice was sincere.

Dylan beamed and her heart warmed. "Oh thank you so much. You're too kind."

Michele flicked her hand in the sharp gesture Dylan was beginning to recognize. "Non! I do not flatter or pander to anyone. If I compliment you, I mean it. If I say nothing, it's because I don't have the praise to give. Simple."

Dylan laughed. "I can respect that. You'd love my sister Sam—she's the same way. I'm very happy you feel more comfortable now and look forward to our next steps."

"To be frank, I'm shocked you haven't gotten further already. Have you tried to get an agent? Your talent is clear." Michele's delicate blonde brows drew together over her elegant straight nose.

Dylan paused and set the computer back on the scarred wooden farm table where she kept some of her supplies. She sat carefully onto the wooden bench before responding.

"Well, for a while I was hesitant because my family's history and publicity. But I have tried to get an agent, and it's so competitive. I do feel like if I can get some exposure, I have a chance to at least make some kind of living at this." Dylan laced her fingers together in her lap.

"May I ask you a frank question again?"

"Of course." Dylan nodded.

"Well, I did some research on your family—please understand I just had to make sure there would be no issues linking our names—and I mean no disrespect. I was sorry to learn about your mother and your reluctance around the paparazzi makes more sense. But why haven't you asked your father to make introductions for you?"

Dylan stiffened. Seriously? She'd researched her? But hell, her dad might have done the same thing if he'd known the unorthodox arrangement with Gabriel. He might actually be making some phone calls right now. At least Michele was nothing but direct.

"Well, I don't want to trade on the McNeill name. Many people want to curry favor with my dad. Would I ever know if they worked with me as a simple favor or if my work actually had any merit? I'd always wonder if it was exhibited because of him."

"How is it different if I am making introductions? I mean, they will know you are engaged to my only son."

Why was Michele asking when she was the one who'd suggested the whole arrangement? Did she want Dylan to consider backing out? "True. But you're an expert in the art world and my dad isn't. Don't people who know you recognize you'd never send them art you didn't like, regardless of Gabriel and me?"

Michele nodded. "Excellent way to respond if anybody asks."

"So, to clarify, you're more like a mentor or role model. And hopefully the link to my family won't be immediate or obvious. It just feels different to me and that's part of why I accepted this…" Dylan gazed out of the enormous windows that lent the perfect natural light for her work.

"*C'est bien*. I understand completely. You are an independent woman and want to do this without feeling your papa is the reason. You and my son have much in common. Well, I think you will be well received. This will be even more publicity, you understand, no?"

"I do. But like I mentioned to Gabriel, it's very different than the type of spotlight he's under. Painters aren't usually splashed across Page Six with the flavor of the day." Dylan bit her lip. Crap, had she just insulted Michele's son to her face?

Michele arched one elegant brow. "That's true. With the end of Gabriel's football career, I think the interest will wane quickly. The press is fickle. But you must be prepared nonetheless."

"*Je comprends.* I understand. We'll keep a low profile." And pray that neither of their families dug too deep.

"Okay. Now, I'll try to see if a show can be arranged soon and we'll all come. His father must see you two together and be convinced you are madly in love and you two must remain in America for the next several months."

Heat rose into Dylan's cheeks–darn fair skin always betrayed her. Although the physical chemistry between them was off the charts, could she and Gabriel act madly in love? What if she actually fell madly in love with him?

Dylan's stomach tensed. Falling in love with Gabriel could break her heart. She'd not forgotten him and hadn't gotten involved seriously with anybody else since Paris. But he wasn't looking for anything beyond finding a way to avoid his dad's plans for him and sharing her bed. Once his leg was better, even if he wasn't playing soccer, she had no doubt all the women would come out of the woodwork for a chance with him again. It wasn't like retired soccer players suddenly became single or settled down with one woman.

"I understand. I hope we can pull it off. Just so you know, I'm not the best at hiding my emotions."

"You'll be fine. My son is intrigued with you and you cannot hide your attraction to him. Again, your chemistry and connection is why I got the marriage idea. I'll make sure that the early exhibition opportunities for you are in the U.S. so you have to remain there." Michele said.

Dylan glanced up at the clock on the far studio wall. Jake and Amanda's engagement party was tonight and she had a long list of tasks to complete before then. "You'll have to excuse me. My sister's engagement party is tonight, so I must run. Shall I call you in a few days or wait to hear from you?"

"I'll be in touch. Enjoy tonight. Perhaps observe your sister with her fiancé and emulate them." Michele gave a small wave and the screen went dark.

Dylan stared at the blank screen and allowed her eyelids to flutter shut. What had she gotten herself into?

Each moment she spent with Gabriel deepened her connection with him. He'd charmed her family at dinner and blown her mind in bed. Day by day and night by tempting night, the fragile boundaries protecting her heart would weaken. Would she begin to believe their fake engagement was real and end up with a broken heart?

Gabriel gripped the armchair so hard it was a miracle it didn't disintegrate into dust. His stomach was coiled in knots, his mouth filled with a bitter taste, and his leg ached like hell. Even after the incredibly satisfying passionate night with Dylan, he'd tossed and turned. Time to find out what the future held.

He gazed between Coach Davis and Bernard LeVeque, his longtime agent/manager. They sat in the Galaxy conference room for the dreaded discussion about his fate. Both their expressions were grim and Davis was having a tough time meeting his eyes. Not a great sign.

"Hit me. Just tell me now." He ground his back molars and tightened his grasp on the chair.

"Okay, Gabriel. As far as your position with the team is concerned, the management has reviewed the surgeon's reports and your prognosis. It's clear you won't be able to play again." Davis paused and cleared his throat. "It's a goddamn shame. We had such high hopes."

Gabriel inhaled deeply and released an unsteady breath. He didn't trust himself to speak. The throbbing pain from his knee leapt to his temples, like someone was pounding on his head with a hammer. It wasn't like he didn't know this, but to hear his coach articulate the words hurt. Hurt worse than the actual injury.

He was only thirty-one years old. No way in hell was he ready to leave his beloved football world.

Bernard piped in. "The good news is we've got some excellent guarantees in your contract. The signing bonus, staggered and guaranteed pay– you'll be pleased. We've also got insurance just in case this happened."

Because Gabriel had literally been within the first month of his tiered five-year contract, he hadn't met some of the milestones required for his entire payout. Not that he really expected to receive $250 million for two matches, but hell, he'd never anticipated getting injured. Bernard worked on commission and wasn't one to leave money on the table. In fact, Bernard had bought a fancy new car and apartment in Paris. So the guy would fight to get Gabriel his due.

He cursed his own ego. Even if you were at the peak of your game, anything could happen. And it had. The asshole who tripped him should pay the lost contract balance.

Gabriel frowned at his agent, who was looking much too relaxed. "What about all my endorsement deals?" He had major ones with several sports companies–everything from watches to cologne to whisky. Not that he needed all the money, but he wasn't going to give it away either.

"No problem. The athletic companies only do one year at a time and the other contracts can continue whether you are playing or retired. Everyone knows who you are and your face will still sell." His agent leaned back and crossed one ankle over his other knee.

As if anyone wanted a has-been like he'd soon be, once the news became public.

"I don't know. I'm more concerned with the sport. And my visa. What's the status with that? If you release me immediately, does that mean I'm on a ticking time clock?" *Mon Dieu*. The vise clenched tighter around his skull.

"Well, there's some ways we can word the paperwork to give you time to figure out your next move. You don't want to head back to Europe once your knee is better? What will you do here?"

Davis asked.

"I don't know." Gabriel roared, unable to restrain himself. "I have no fucking clue what I'm going to do, but I want to stay here. I left my country to come here and I'm not ready to move back." Not ready to battle my father over the family business.

Bernard held up his hands and Davis's eyes were huge in his weathered face. Gabriel didn't usually pitch fits. He wasn't a prima donna, part of the reason he had earned such a big contract. Not only was he the best in the world, he was also relatively reasonable.

As long as he got his way, which hadn't ever been a problem before.

"I know you're upset. Sorry. I know everything happened really fast. We'll deal with the visa, at least for a while, okay?" Bernard's tone was irritatingly soothing.

"How?" Gabriel's nostrils flared and he gritted his teeth. Had Bernard always sounded so condescending? Because right now he was getting on his last nerve.

"Look, I'll talk to the GM, okay? We'll work on it." Davis interjected. "There is another thing. I was going to wait, but since you said you want to stay..." He shrugged his shoulders and lifted his hands.

"What? Just ask me now." How much worse could it get?

"I was talking with the rest of the management team and we all agreed that you would be an incredible mentor and coach for the front line. Have you ever thought about coaching?"

Gabriel's jaw dropped. "You want me to go to practices, stand on the sidelines, and watch others play in my spot? Are you kidding me?"

Davis shook his head. "I knew it was too soon. I'm sorry. Gabriel, part of your success is because of the way your mind works, the strategies, and the instincts that don't come naturally to 99% of the players. You had to have considered that for when you retired, right?"

Gabriel shook his head. "I live in the present. My whole world was these five years. This season. Everything after that seemed far away. My success is because I do focus on the present and not worry about what might happen later." And wasn't that life strategy biting him in the ass right now.

Bernard stood, suddenly not quite so laconic. "I've thought about it and I have other ideas."

"What ideas?" Gabriel quirked a brow.

"Well, you pay me to manage your career, oui? Of course I have thought about your retirement. I just thought it would be several years away. But I have ideas that may be more appealing to you than coaching other players." Bernard's fox-like features sharpened, his small coffee-colored eyes narrowing on Gabriel's face.

"Listen to him, Gabriel. I know I'm curious." Davis said.

Gabriel threw up his hands. "Fine. What?" Damn it, he wasn't supposed to be having this discussion. Not now. Not yet.

"Okay, hear me out. You're one of the players who have helped lift football, real football, up into the public's awareness in America. They love you here. You're articulate, charming, and like Davis said, you've got one of the keenest tactical minds in the game." His agent paused and cracked his knuckles.

"And?" He wasn't following. Not with the pounding headache and the reality of all of this slamming into him like a ton of concrete.

"You're like a wet dream for the sports networks. With you as a commentator and a face of the game, you'd draw in even more people to the sport. You could work on games here, tournaments, go back to Europe and work for FIFA, the Olympics–the sky is the limit. It just depends on if you want to stay here or split your time or whatever." Bernard approached and leaned over him.

Gabriel threw his hands up again. A television commentator? "Again, that's being on the sidelines."

"Well, you won't be on the field again. The sooner you accept it, the better." Bernard retreated and sat back in his chair.

As if he knew that Gabriel was close to exploding.

"It's been a little over a week. I've played my whole life." Was he just supposed to be like, oh fine, that's over. Never mind. Bullshit.

"Gabriel–you've got plenty of time. Don't worry. I'll work with legal on the timing of releasing you from the team. I know I can get you at least six months. You don't have to decide anything right now. But I have to agree with Bernard." Davis smiled, but kept his distance.

Smart move–Gabriel was close to erupting. Although his temper took a while to ignite, it had been simmering since he'd ended up in the hospital. All this talk about his future and jobs and immigration issues was too damn much.

Six months: Time to figure out what he'd do here in the States. Wasn't Bernard's suggestion exactly why he'd agreed to his mother's proposition?

Six months: Time for his sister to prove herself with a new vintage and sway their father's stubborn viewpoint.

Six months: Time for Dylan to get discovered as an artist. Living a lie with Dylan and her family had him on edge. Sure, everything was incredible when they were alone, but if her family suspected anything, their entire plan would combust.

"Gabriel?" Bernard's voice had returned to that grating sycophantic tone.

Gabriel gathered himself. If he didn't let off some steam, he would blow. Without the physical release of running and training and kicking his beloved black and white ball, he was boiling over with spiraling thoughts and rapid mood swings.

Damn it, he needed to do something today before he exploded.

"I need a drink. I can't discuss this anymore." Too much, too soon.

"I get it. It'll work out. Sorry Gabriel." Coach

Davis pushed to his feet. His lanky form revealed his own athletic past. "I'll be in touch soon. In the meantime, do live in the present and focus on your recovery. And get a damn shot or three of whisky. You deserve it." He patted Gabriel's shoulder and crossed the room to the exit.

"Whisky it is. And I won't bring any of this up again today. There's a dive bar around the corner. Let's go drown some of this out." Bernard picked up Gabriel's crutches.

Tonight was Dylan's sister Amanda's engagement party. And they had to put on a show like a truly loving couple for the McNeills and all their friends. He glanced at his watch. It was only 2 p.m.

Enough time for a few drinks to take off the edge and still be back down in Rancho Santa Fe on schedule. Bernard could drive him back before 5 p.m.

Plenty of time.

CHAPTER 16

DYLAN HISSED IN FRUSTRATION, TOSSED back her flute of rosé champagne, and slapped the glass onto the granite countertop in the guest-house's open kitchen. So much for the romantic pre-party with her fake fiancé she'd planned.

She snatched up her phone, glanced down at the dark screen, and rolled her eyes skyward. No replies to her three texts and two phone calls. Crickets. Damn him. Amanda and Jake's engagement party started at six and it was already 5:47 p.m. He was perfectly aware tonight was their second major performance as lovebirds. It wasn't like the party was a surprise.

At five o'clock, Dylan was mildly annoyed, but assumed he'd been delayed in one of his meetings. Hell, she'd thought after last night, he'd hurry back. He'd indicated as much this morning when he'd made them breakfast, whipping up a delicious omelet, prepared how only the French can prepare eggs.

At five-thirty, her temper kicked in. Hell, she'd been soaring on Cloud Nine all day anticipating a little afternoon delight, maybe a shower together

so she could make sure he didn't injure his leg further—now she'd crashed back to earth. So much
for presenting a united front.

She stalked back to the master bedroom to fetch
her small plum-colored satin clutch and freshen
her lipstick. The mirror reflected two flags of scar-
let slashing across her cheekbones and no, it was
not overzealously applied blush. Nope, her fair
skin revealed the early signs of her fury—but she
refused to allow her black mood to ruin Amanda's
night.

She took a cleansing breath and smoothed down
the perfect flounce of ruffles of her off-the-shoul-
der bodice. The silky white dress splashed with
violet flowers hugged her form down to her hips,
showing off her slender waist, before flaring out
into a full skirt that skimmed her ankles. Dark pur-
ple wedge heels with ankle strap ribbons boosted
her 5'2 height. All in all, she looked pretty darn
spectacular, if she did say so herself.

Gabriel, had he deigned to grace her with his
presence, had a shirt with a white and deep blue
pattern that would coordinate perfectly, along
with a borrowed pair of Holt's cowboy boots
because he'd balked at getting his own. One more
sign he wasn't all the way into their arrangement.
He needed boots to live on the ranch. She snorted.

If her family suspected something was amiss,
especially if her father's usual keen instincts
detected a problem, she'd strangle Gabriel. Damn
it, now she'd just have to lie again—why not, when
she was living a damn lie— and say he'd been

caught in L.A. traffic. Nobody would question it. She practiced her four-part breath to prevent her emotions from obliterating her rational side.

She marched to the large mahogany front door and yanked it open. She yelped and jumped back.

Sam stood in the doorway, her expression thunderous. Her twin's temper was notorious and her short fuse appeared ready to detonate. Despite her long auburn hair spilling over her shoulders, her pale pink Western shirt, dressy jeans, and fancy white boots, she didn't look like a joyous sibling attending her sister's engagement celebration. She looked like she was about to murder someone. Uh-oh.

Sam thrust her phone into her face. "What the *hell* does your fiancé think he's doing?"

Dylan retreated another step. "I can't see the screen when it's against the tip of my nose. What's going on?"

"Well, your *fiancé*," Sam drawled out the word and made air quotes, "Your fiancé's just been photographed getting drunk in some dive bar in L.A. at a table surrounded by a gaggle of half-naked women. He looks wasted. What the hell is going on?"

Dylan grabbed the phone out of her sister's hand and scrolled through the gossip rag's report. "You've got to be kidding me. Does this say what time this is?" Her blood started pulsating in her veins and her hands began to tremble.

"I couldn't tell, but it is today. I thought he was up at a business meeting?" Sam's dark brows drew together.

"Oh my god. He hasn't returned my calls or texts. I figured his meetings ran over. Which doesn't excuse it, but this is b.s." Dylan couldn't pretend with her twin sister.

Only her true attraction to Gabriel prevented her sister from suspecting too much about the speedy engagement. But she wasn't going to be able to fool Samantha if he was going to mess up like this.

"Well, he's obviously been drinking a while because he looks plastered and I for one don't appreciate him sitting with all these women when he's supposed to be here with you. You better hope Dad doesn't see this." Sam's scowled.

Dylan's shoulders drooped. Was she such a sentimental sap to believe Gabriel would be different with her? Charming guys like him, professional athletes who were used to everyone fawning over them, wouldn't have an easy time changing their ways. But, she'd thought he might be genuine. Argh. Sure, the engagement was a sham, but he needed the subterfuge more than she did. Selfish ass.

She drew herself up to her full height. "Let's go."

"How are you going to explain his absence?" Sam demanded.

"I'm just going to say he got delayed in L.A. for team business. Nobody else needs to know I haven't heard from him and he's off getting drunk. The jerk." Dylan blew out an unsteady breath.

"Back me up?"

"Of course I have your back. But you and I are talking later because something isn't right here. I don't know what it is, but you *will* share with me sooner or later."

Dylan frowned. Maybe she should just confide in her twin. She could trust Sam. But how could she ever admit this ridiculous predicament she'd entangled herself in?

"There's nothing to share. But let's do this, okay?"

Sam reached for her hand and squeezed. Her large brown eyes showed her concern. "Okay. For now. Let's go put on the best party in the world for Amanda. If Gabriel makes it back, fine. But I'll act like it's not a big deal and help you out."

Dylan tried for a smile. "Thank you. Let's grab another glass of champagne for the walk to help soothe my nerves. You can drink from Gabriel's glass since he didn't bother to show up."

She scooted back to the kitchen, filled both glasses to the rim, and tucked her anger to the back corner of her heart to be dealt with later.

Gabriel continued to ignore the overly tanned brunette on his left side. Why were these women at he and Bernard's table? He wasn't in the mood to talk to anyone; much less these groupies who just wanted to get their photograph in the paper with a famous athlete.

A flash went off and he jolted in his seat, covering his eyes with his arm to avoid getting blinded. *Zut.* He glanced up and sure enough, some bearded guy dressed like a lumberjack was snapping photos. He grabbed Bernard's arm and addressed him in French.

"We've got to leave. The last thing we need is photos of me in this bar at lunchtime." Gabriel's tongue felt thick in his mouth.

Bernard nodded, but appeared unconcerned. "Don't worry. It's not a big deal and it's definitely not anywhere close to lunchtime."

Gabriel shook his head, his thoughts muddled. Bernard's voice seemed like it was coming from far away. Despite only sipping a couple of whiskies, he felt out of control–a condition he usually avoided. He'd never been fall down drunk and prided himself on his restraint.

"I must be back in Rancho Santa Fe by five o'clock and we've got to miss traffic. You're okay to drive me, right?" Bernard was drinking club soda with lime.

"Well, that's not going to happen, mon ami. It's already 4:20 p.m. and we're going to hit rush hour. Why don't we get an early supper and I'll drive you back afterward."

Gabriel slammed his hand down on the weathered wooden table. "What? You knew I had to be back for my fiancée's sister's fête. Why'd you let me stay here this long?" Despite the fuzziness in his brain, anger filled him.

Bernard shrugged. "Look, today you got some tough news. I'm just trying to be here as your friend and not just your agent. You needed a few drinks."

"Look. You knew I had to get back." Gabriel gritted his teeth. His mouth felt like he had a mountain of sand in it. What the hell was in that whisky? He'd only had two. Not enough to feel this way.

"Can't you tell time too? I'll get the bill and we'll leave. I'll get you back, okay?" Bernard shoved to his feet and strode to the bar.

Gabriel used the thick table under his hands and surged to his feet. He winced once his foot hit the sticky bar floor. *Damn it.* He glanced around for his crutches.

"Oh, let me help you." The brunette next to him cooed and pulled the crutches out from underneath the table.

He'd forgotten she was still there. Thank goodness he and Bernard had been speaking French. Not that she'd know what they were talking about, but he didn't need gossip.

"Merci. Thank you." He managed a smile at her and wondered about the habit of so many of these American women to ruin their faces with over-inflated lips and frozen foreheads. You didn't see this phenomenon much in Europe.

A flash blinded him again. Mon Dieu, he would kill this asshole who kept photographing him. He'd probably caught him smiling at this woman, both of their hands on his crutches.

Bernard returned to his side and shielded Gabriel from the photographer as he hobbled out of the bar. Luckily, Bernard's car was nearby in the parking garage and no other paparazzi were outside. If only the guy hadn't been inside.

He managed to fumble his way to the car. Threw his crutches in the back and adjusted himself into the front seat. He'd scooted it back far enough his leg could stretch out.

"Don't worry. I'm going get you some coffee and we'll be back before you know it. We should be able to take the carpool lane most of the way. You'll be fine."

Gabriel shrugged and pulled out his phone, which he'd never bothered to power back on after the meeting. All he'd wanted was a drink to soften his new reality, a.k.a. the implosion of his life. *Merde*. Several texts popped up and most were from Dylan.

He thunked his head against the headrest and groaned. She was furious and rightly so. A damn gossip site had already published a photo of he and Bernard at a table with the women. Somehow, he looked like he was having the time of his life, drinking away the afternoon, a party guy on a twenty-four-hour bender. *Merde. Merde. Merde.* How did these guys get these photos? His mother would kill him if she saw them and his dad would never buy the engagement story.

"Is your leg okay? You in pain?" Bernard asked as he wove through traffic.

Gabriel shifted his focus to his knee. "It's not so bad. Those pain pills must be really strong."

He straightened in his seat. The pain pills. No

wonder he'd zoned out and lost track of time. Although he'd weaned his dosage to a minimum, the drugs were powerful, especially followed by hard alcohol on an empty stomach. Damn it, now he looked like a total asshole and he couldn't blame Dylan for being furious.

How could he have forgotten to send her a text after the meeting at least? He was going to miss the beginning of the engagement party. The party where they were supposed to convince all the people how in love they were and how excited they were to plan their own wedding.

He was in a terrible position.

Her family had been kind and welcoming, but he would bet Mr. McNeill wouldn't be thrilled to see him roll in late.

"You can come in with me while I shower and change and then drop me up at the main house, right? I can't walk up there and I don't want to ask Dylan to come back down for me. She's already angry."

"Sure. Whatever you need. You okay?"

"Yeah. Just realized I'd taken pain pills this morning and mixing with the whisky wasn't so smart. Let me text her and see if I can start diffusing the situation."

Bernard chuckled. "You're excellent at calming women down. She'll be fine."

"She's different. This is all on me." His gut tightened.

Bernard just nodded and focused on driving.

Gabriel sucked in a breath and typed out a reply.

I'm really sorry. I can explain. I'll be there as soon as I can.

Dylan didn't reply.

So much for their sexy morning setting the tone for the rest of the day. He put his phone down, closed his eyes, and leaned his head back. Time to rest before he arrived because he had some groveling to do.

All the groveling.

CHAPTER 17

"**H**E'S HERE WITH THAT GUY from the bar." Sam hissed in Dylan's ear. "You should go over and meet him. Act overjoyed to see him and rip him a new one when you guys are alone later."

Dylan narrowed her eyes across the sea of people sipping cocktails and swaying to the mellow tune filling the soft summer air. Her breath lodged in her throat. He looked gorgeous in the Western button down, the crisp white and vibrant blue plaid setting off his bronzed skin. The wooden crutches supported his lean body while his feline green eyes skimmed the crowd, searching.

When his gaze caught hers, she plastered on what she hoped could be taken for a loving smile and strolled in his direction. She took her sweet time crossing the pool area and the clubhouse they'd transformed into a beautiful bower of flowers, complete with a temporary dance floor, a DJ spinning tunes, cocktail stations, and a full buffet.

No way would she trot over to him like an eager puppy yearning for attention. He was the late one and he could wait for her now. A lanky, sandy haired man wearing wire-rimmed glasses stood next to him. His agent?

"Darling, you made it." She practically cooed the words like a loving fiancée, but the sweet tone didn't reflect in her eyes.

His gaze didn't waver from hers and his lips curved up. "I am sorry to be so late. I can explain…"

His smile faltered. If her eyes were truly the windows to her soul, he would be quaking in his borrowed boots. *Good, he should be worried.* Although anyone glancing at them would only be able to see two lovers reuniting as she stepped in and kissed him.

"We'll discuss this later and you better pray nobody else in the family saw those photos of you with your…your friends." She murmured the words against his lips, and then stepped back. Ignored the electric jolt that happened every time they touched.

"Please don't be angry with Gabriel. It was a tough morning and I insisted we have a drink." The guy next to him held out one hand.

Dylan glanced down. Ignoring the gesture would be childish, so she shook his hand. "And you are?"

He clasped her hand with both of his, his dark eyes pleading. "Bernard LeVeque. I am Gabriel's agent and manager. I should have paid better attention to the time and also remembered he had taken some pain pills today. It is all my fault. I've already made some calls to get the photos taken down. *Je suis désole.*"

Pain pills and whisky weren't exactly a winning combination. Could it really have just been a mistake? She looked at Gabriel again and he was so damn handsome, her heart slammed against her ribcage. Dangerous. Although she'd entered their arrangement with open eyes and believed she could handle being friends with benefits, her heart was more involved than she cared to admit.

Damn it, seeing him smiling at those women had been like a knife twisting in her gut.

Especially after last night.

"Gabriel's an adult, but thanks for your explanation. Did you want to stay for a drink? Something to eat?" She smiled at him, no need to shoot the messenger. And wouldn't she be friendly to her "fiancé's" agent?

But Bernard was shaking his head. "Non, non, I must return to L.A. tonight. But merci, I can see now why Gabriel fell for you so quickly and wants to marry you." He flashed a charming grin.

"You sure?" Gabriel glanced at him.

"Of course. Have a lovely night and again, I apologize." With that, he turned on his heel and walked away, leaving them alone.

For a moment, they stared at each other. "Do you want to get something to eat first? And I'm assuming you're drinking water tonight?" And there was the forceful tone, but too bad. She wasn't a saint.

"Dylan, I know you're disappointed with me. This morning was really rough and I needed a whisky. I just wish I'd remembered about the damn meds. It won't happen again." His thick brows drew together.

"Well, you sound fine now." And of course he looked mouthwateringly hot.

"That's good, non?" His mouth twitched. "A freezing cold shower and two cups of black coffee helped. If anyone notices, we can blame it on my recent operation, non?"

Her heart softened at the reminder. He had just gotten major surgery and lost his dream career in a span of a few weeks. She couldn't imagine how difficult it would be to actually have achieved your pinnacle career and have it yanked from you in a flash.

But this was a reminder not to count on him too much. He had the power to break her heart and she wouldn't allow that to happen. "I'm sorry it was rough and I do want to hear what happened later. For now, we need to make the rounds, well as much as you can on crutches. Let's go over to the buffet and get you some dinner."

"Merci." He flashed his white teeth and her stomach fluttered. His easy charm threatened her equilibrium.

They wove through the crowd, with only a few meet and greets along the way. The focus tonight was on Amanda and Jake. Dylan ignored the questioning gazes. She wasn't sure how many people knew of their engagement, but it had been on the news. God, she hoped his afternoon exploits hadn't been seen by anybody. At least not tonight.

They reached the expansive tables laden with platters of food and decorated with lush vases of colorful flowers, where Amanda was chatting with Owen and Marco. The two ranch managers were essential parts of the team who helped run Pacific Vista Ranch's successful horse-breeding operation.

"Gabriel, you made it. Is everything okay?" Amanda smiled, her eyes warm—an excellent indicator she had not seen the damning photos.

Her fake fiancé nodded and flashed his million-dollar grin. "Please accept my apologies. Congratulations. Where's your lucky guy?"

She waved her slender hand. "He's getting us another drink. Have you met Owen, our stallion manager, and Marco, our head groom yet?"

The guys all shook hands and exchanged pleasantries. Amanda raised a brow and Dylan shrugged. No need to give her sister anything to think about besides her special evening.

Jake stepped up next to Amanda, leaned down for a quick tender kiss, and handed her a glass of white wine. "Hey Gabriel, Dylan."

Jake was a man of few words. He slid one brawny arm around her sister's slender form and hugged her into his side. Happiness glowed on both their faces—because they were actually in love and engaged for real. Imagine that.

Earlier this year, Jake had rescued a dog from a hit and run accident near the ranch and brought her up for Amanda to save. They hadn't seen each other since she'd been his math tutor in high school. His unrequited freshman crush blossomed into true love. Stella, the dog who'd brought them together, was now their fur baby.

"I'm going to make a plate for Gabriel so he can sit down for a bit." Dylan ignored the pang in her chest. She was thrilled for her sister and Jake, but it made it harder to pretend to be in love with Gabriel. A few moments alone at the food table would help her gather the necessary energy to act affectionate.

"Of course. Jake, will you grab Gabriel a drink and I'll keep him company until Dylan's finished?" Amanda smiled up at her firefighter husband-to-be.

"Just a sparkling water, please." Gabriel set his crutches aside and sank into one of the chairs at the round table next to them.

Amanda's brows rose, but she didn't say anything. Jake just nodded and headed back to the bar. Owen and Marco followed him, empty glasses in hand.

Dylan bit the inside of her lip. She needed to pull it together and act normal. Loving and normal. "I'll be right back." She blew a kiss to Gabriel who returned the gesture.

Gabriel's temples throbbed and his knee ached like hell. Right about now, he would kill to be reclining on the guesthouse's comfortable couch with an icepack on his knee and a cloth over his eyes.

"You're feeling terrible Gabriel, aren't you?" Amanda's voice was low and sympathetic.

"Terrible?" He snapped his head toward her and prayed she was asking about his knee and couldn't see the guilt weighing on him from the disastrous afternoon.

"I can see that you're hurting, even though you're really good at hiding it."

"And you can tell?" Damn, so much for his acting skills.

She nodded with a wry smile. "You forget–I have to read horses' minds and figure out what's wrong with them. It's a skill. Are you on still on medication?"

"Oui, yes. But I've been weaning off and·hope to stop in the next few days. They wanted me to finish the one prescription."

"Makes sense. Don't feel like you have to stay too long this evening–rest is important. Has Dylan given you the full tour of the ranch? I know it's tough because you can't ride or walk around yet."

"Not yet. I was in Los Angeles longer than I'd planned today. Maybe tomorrow. What I've seen is gorgeous."

"There's nowhere like it." She smiled again. "Dylan mentioned you grew up on a vineyard in the South of France? I'm assuming that wasn't too tough."

He winced. "Sablet, my hometown, is heaven. The weather is similar to yours and some of the vegetation as well. But every place and every family has its challenges, *n'est-ce pas?*" *Like overbearing fathers who believe it is still 1895.*

Jake approached with his drink and placed one large hand on Amanda's shoulder. "Rafe's here with a date and he says he needs you to meet her. You know, for approval." His lips twitched.

Amanda laughed. "Rafe is Jake's big brother and his dating choices are legendary. Maybe this one will be a contender." She rose from the table.

"Dylan should be back soon, Gabriel. I've got to mingle and check on Jake's older brother. He can be a...bad picker. For some reason he believes I'm a great judge of character."

"No doubt you are. Congratulations again." Amanda was lovely and seemed to like him so far, so that was a plus. Did she approve of him being engaged to her little sister?

They strolled off, Jake's brawny arm cradling Amanda against his side. What did true love feel like?

A few short weeks ago, he'd only been interested in rekindling his affair with Dylan based on one hot night together. Seeing her again and starting to date her had seemed like the perfect scenario. Focus on their careers and enjoy their free time together. Simple.

He'd thought his career had no end—had truly never considered what came after he could no longer score goals and lead his team to victory. Nor had he considered a relationship that went beyond the moment—all his energy had been dedicated to his beloved football.

Now he didn't have a clue what he was going

to do with the rest of his life, but he'd make sure nobody decided for him. Making this engagement seem real until they'd each achieved what they needed from their bargain was key. He needed to figure out a way to apologize to Dylan for today, because if she remained angry with him, nobody would buy their story.

He wanted to be worthy of Dylan, even if the situation was temporary.

Once Dylan had her dreams fulfilled, he'd be extraneous.

Suddenly, Dylan set a fragrant overflowing plate down in front of him. She dropped silverware and a napkin next to it and sank into the seat Amanda had just vacated. Her pale throat worked as she swallowed a large sip of champagne and instantly he was aroused.

"Merci. You look incredible tonight." And she did. Her beauty slammed into him, from the creamy skin and full red lips to her enormous doe eyes. Even though those dark depths didn't hold much warmth at the current moment.

She merely raised her dark brows. "You should eat."

Gabriel glanced down at the food. He wasn't hungry. Right now, all he wanted was to go back twenty-four hours to when they were having an intimate, playful evening together. Damn it. His life was a rollercoaster right now and he couldn't seem to find any solid ground.

Time to turn it around. "This looks incredible." Crispy fried chicken, plump red tomatoes and sliced cucumbers, a mound of mashed potatoes, and a few slices of watermelon looked like enough food to feed them both. Now there was an idea.

He speared some tomato and cucumber on his fork and held it toward her lips. "You first."

Dylan leaned back in her chair and crossed her arms. "Sorry, I already ate. This is for you."

Zut. "What can I do? I've already apologized and I'm truly sorry. How can I make it up to you?" What he wouldn't give to have her eyes soft like melted chocolate, like they'd been last night.

"Look, Gabriel. I'm not happy. I can't just switch my emotions on and off like a faucet. You let me down and we're barely into our bargain. I don't know how we can make this work when it's starting off this way. We might just need to forget about it." She frowned and shook her head.

He reached out and covered her slender hand with his. She didn't yank it away, so that was progress. "I know. But please give me another chance. You and I both have a lot to gain from this. I swear I won't screw up again." *He hoped.* It wasn't like he had his crap together.

Dylan sipped more champagne. "You're right. I had a good talk with your mother this morning. I'll give you one more chance. But this is truly going to be pretend from now on. I cannot do this and sleep with you."

And what exactly did that mean? "Will we not sleep in the same bed? Weren't you worried about one of your family dropping by and discovering us sleeping in different rooms?"

Dylan's full lips flattened. "Fine. But it's a California King. You'll sleep on your side and I'll sleep on mine. And if you try anything, you're sleeping in a guest room. We can just say you couldn't rest because of your knee and went in the other room. Got it?"

Gabriel reached for her hand again. How in hell was he expected to pull back after what they'd already shared? Sure, he'd been late and sure, he should have texted her, but damn. Her jaw was set, so he wouldn't insist. Not yet anyway. But no way was their relationship going to stay platonic. He'd make it up to her.

"Got it. Now we need to mingle tonight, right? Make sure everyone notices us together, especially your family?"

Dylan turned her hand over and squeezed his. "Yes. But after you eat. Everyone knows you're on crutches, so we have that on our side." She scooted her chair closer to him.

Her honeyed scent wafted toward his nostrils and every single one of his muscles stiffened. He'd rather gobble her up than all this food on his plate. Her passionate nature tempted him beyond measure. Beyond what he'd ever experienced.

He'd not screw up again.

"Deal. While I eat, please tell me about your call with my maman. Does she have anything set up for you yet? Will she focus on California first or New York or Paris?"

Dylan's face lit up. Gabriel's fingers tightened on his fork.

Focus on the meal.
Focus on the discussion.
Focus on Dylan.

"We had the best conversation. She's amazing. I showed her some of my work and she was really encouraging. Said she felt confident I'd get some bites." She gestured with her hands and once again he was struck by the strength in her long slender fingers. She could be French too, with the way she spoke with her expressive hands.

He nodded. Good, she was starting to relax. He shoved a bite of chicken into his mouth and groaned when the flavors exploded on his tongue. It wasn't a dish he'd had before, but it was delectable.

Dylan's lips curved up. "Excellent, right? We had the party catered, but Angela insisted on making the chicken. Nobody's can compare to hers."

"Delicious. Your stepmother is gifted. I'm so glad my mom sees your talent. I know she liked you, but her believing in your art will truly make her want to help you." He paused and sampled the fluffy whipped potatoes.

"I hope so. I just want the chance. That's all. Just the chance." She gazed down and the fan of her thick dark lashes contrasted against her creamy skin.

"I understand." He reached for her hand again and squeezed. He wanted nothing more than for her to succeed. Nothing compared to living the life of your dreams. To making them reality.

His gut clenched. Would he ever experience that

feeling again? But now wasn't the time to brood. Now was the time for he and Dylan to persuade the world they were truly an engaged couple. He had the rest of his life to relive his football career and replay that moment on the field that ended it all.

"There you are. Nice of you to show up." Samantha said, a thread of sarcasm lacing her tone. Gabriel looked up. Holt and Sam slid into two empty chairs at the table.

Holt smiled at him and winked. "So the boots work? Feel like a cowboy yet?"

Thank god he had an ally in Holt because Sam might be the one person they'd have trouble convincing. But if he just focused on his attraction to Dylan, he wouldn't have to fake anything. He'd never felt so drawn to a woman in his life.

"I don't know about feeling like a cowboy, but I kind of like them." He grinned and interlaced his fingers with Dylan's.

"Have you guys seen dad yet? And Grant's here." Sam's tone softened a bit.

"No way. I can't wait to see Grant." Dylan's eyes widened. "We've been over here since Gabriel arrived. What about Austin and Ryan?"

"Yes, all three of them are here. They're all over by the pool house with dad and Angela." Sam nodded. "Gabriel, has Dylan told you much about our stepbrothers?"

Gabriel smiled back at Sam. "Of course. Grant's the married one who has been living in Melbourne, right?" Dylan had briefed him well.

Sam's jaw relaxed a millimeter. "Yeah, but his wife isn't here."

"Well I hope he's okay staying at the house since we're in the guesthouse" Dylan finished the last sip of her champagne and stood. "We're going to go say hi to the family."

"There are some couches Gabriel, so you won't have to spend too much time on your leg." Sam's smile was genuine now.

Gabriel cursed the awkwardness of the crutches because he wasn't able to have an arm around Dylan or even hold hands while they crossed the crowded party. He gritted his teeth. They reached the pool house, a medium-sized bungalow covered with strands of sparkling lights. An enormous L-shaped beige couch with an ottoman beckoned to him. His knee was throbbing like a bitch.

"Rest here. I'll grab us drinks and find my parents and Grant. Don't ask him about his wife because I'm not sure why she isn't with him." Dylan reached up and clasped his cheeks and pressed her soft lips against his. She tasted like strawberries and champagne.

He loved strawberries and champagne.

Before he could deepen the kiss, she sauntered off toward the bar. He sank into the plush cushions and propped his leg up on the ottoman. If walking for two minutes caused this much pain, staying in America for several months of the best rehab his money could buy was inevitable.

"Gabriel, there you are. Where's Dylan?" Angela appeared next to him, with Chris at her side.

"Hello Chris, Angela." He smiled broadly at them both. "Dylan is getting drinks. She should be right back." Neither one was glaring at him, so they hadn't seen this afternoon's disastrous photos. Hopefully Bernard could get them removed. His shoulders relaxed.

"How are you feeling?" Chris's brow creased.

"Okay." Gabriel shrugged. "I wanted to compliment you, Angela. Your chicken was the best I've ever had. It might be my new favorite food."

She beamed. "Thanks. Sunday nights are family dinners, but you and Dylan are welcome to come up any evening."

"Here you go, sweetie." Dylan returned, handed him his sparkling water, and nestled into the crook of his arm on the couch.

"Well Grant's looking for you, so I'll send him over here. You'll be here for a bit?" Chris's brow arched.

Dylan nodded. "Yes, send him over. I can't wait to see him."

Once they'd left, Dylan turned and kissed him again. He shifted and pulled her into his arms, his hands sliding up her back to tangle in her thick, silky auburn mane. He groaned when her lips parted against his and deepened the kiss.

"A-hem." The sound of a man clearing his throat filtered in through the haze of desire clouding his brain. "Dylan?"

Gabriel shifted back and Dylan reluctantly broke the kiss with a small hum in the back of her throat. Damn, she was sexy.

She popped off the couch and threw herself into the arms of a tall muscular guy with dark hair, who spun her around in a circle. He'd better be her stepbrother.

The guy placed her back on her feet and stepped forward and offered his hand. "Hey Gabriel, Grant Michaels. I'm a big fan of yours. Can't believe you're engaged to my baby sister."

Grant was a good-looking guy with a square jaw and golden brown eyes. He looked friendly so far. "Thanks. Your sister is incredible. Dylan tells me you live in Australia?"

Grant's smile faded and he nodded. "I've lived all over and Australia's the latest."

Dylan smiled and patted her stepbrother's shoulder. "Grant's the nomad in the family. You okay? You look tired."

"Thanks. But yeah, I just got in today and the time change is never easy. I'm going to turn in, but looking forward to getting to know you." Grant said.

"Of course. We'll catch up later."

Dylan's stepbrother strode off in the direction of the main house.

"How about you and I sneak off to our place. You actually look more tired than Grant. We've seen and been seen, so let's get you to bed." Dylan's velvety voice whispered in his ear.

And he was rock hard. "Give me a second and I'll be ready to go."

Dylan smiled down at him. "Even though we kissed tonight, don't think you're doing anything more than sleeping in the same bed with me. That was for show."

Her smile belied the sting in her words.

So much for a full reconciliation tonight. But he could wait. It wasn't like he had a job or anywhere to go right now.

CHAPTER 18

DYLAN SPOONED EXTRA COFFEE INTO the French press, desperate for caffeine after a restless night. Gabriel had tossed and turned, unable to get comfortable with his swollen bandaged knee. His discomfort and inability to sleep had kept her up as well. Although she'd threatened to banish him to the guest room because of his screw-up yesterday, it might be a practical necessity so she could get some rest.

Seeing him wince and hearing him curse under his breath was a big reminder of exactly how much his life had changed. Sure, she was still irritated with him for being late yesterday, but her heart ached for him. His entire life had been shattered, not just his leg. And while it probably hadn't been the smartest choice to have drinks after his devastating business meeting, could she blame him? At about 3 a.m. she'd concluded she couldn't be angry with him about the paparazzi photos. Not when she knew how that world worked.

The timing had simply been terrible.

She gazed out the window over the kitchen sink, admiring the varying shades of blue coloring the morning sky. This time, she'd give him the benefit of the doubt. The temptation presented by his mother's introductions was significant. But she'd remember that she needed to protect her heart from him. Because their evening together the other night had been incredible and intimate. Much more than a simple hook up. Recalling the pit in her belly yesterday reminded her to not let him get too close and focus on what mattered.

Coordinating with Michele about other opportunities.

Continuing to contact Laguna galleries.

Convincing her family and the world at large that she and Gabriel were in love.

A few weeks ago, these would have been her biggest challenges, but now hiding her burgeoning feelings for the French heartthrob was priority number one. Hell, the angst would transfer well to canvas just like it had back after her mother died when she was fifteen. Channeling her heartbreak had not just been therapeutic, but had confirmed painting was her true calling.

"Bonjour, beautiful." Gabriel rasped from just behind her.

The hairs on the nape of her neck leapt to attention. How had he managed to sneak up on her? She turned away from the window and he was leaning against the granite countertop, wearing only his loose-fitting drawstring cotton sweats.

"You startled me. How did you get in here so quietly? Where are your crutches?" She swallowed. His bare bronzed muscular chest beckoned to be touched–too tempting.

"Those torture devices are still in the bedroom. I hopped on one leg. Please tell me you made enough café for me too?" His green eyes were heavy-lidded, evidencing his sleepless night.

"Of course. And I made it twice as strong as usual for you." She poured the midnight black brew and handed him the cup. "Please sit down–you're not supposed to put any weight on your leg."

He grimaced. "You're right. I hate this." He limped to the small kitchen table tucked into a corner.

She busied herself adding oat milk to her coffee. "I was about to make myself some scrambled eggs. Can I make you some?"

"Please. I don't want you to feel you need to wait on me or cook for me though. That's not part of our deal." He gazed up at her, his handsome face drawn in tight lines.

Her stomach twisted at the word "deal"–as if she could forget this was a business transaction. If she were more like her pragmatic older sister Amanda, she might have been less impetuous about agreeing to this unorthodox liaison. Any potential for a real relationship went up in flames once he'd been injured and needed her help. This fake engagement could only end one way and it wasn't happily ever after.

For better or for worse. No pun intended. "Let's not worry about that right now. Okay?"

He reached out a hand to her. "Dylan."

She crossed the few steps to him and accepted his hand, her entire body heating at the contact, like it did each time they touched. He tugged gently and pulled her onto his lap. The warmth from his smooth muscular chest and the dark scruff on his square jaw competed for her attention. Good lord. How could she maintain boundaries around him?

He kept her hand clasped in his and with his other hand brushed his long fingers along her cheek, then tilted her chin to meet his kiss. His lips were feather light and more devastating for the tenderness. She melted against him, careful not to let her weight shift onto his injured leg.

"You're an angel. The way I feel about you is not part of a business arrangement, okay?" He murmured the words against her lips, his warm breath mingling with hers.

Her pulse skipped a beat in her chest. Falling back on her innate ability to flirt, she smiled against his mouth and asked, "And how do you feel?"

His hand slid from her jaw up to cup the back of her head, the pressure from his fingers firm against her scalp. "You know I find you incredibly sexy, but I also find you kind and compassionate and loyal. And once you show me your paintings today, I know I'll find you to be talented as well."

Her eyelids fluttered shut and she melted against him. His seductive whisper was turning her bones to liquid. She was an adult—she could handle their physical relationship and keep her heart separate, couldn't she? She'd withdrawn from prior relationships when her emotions became too tangled. Nobody had captured her heart.

She couldn't resist him.

She didn't want to resist him.

She angled her mouth and deepened their kiss. If she took charge, she'd be fine. He growled low in his throat and clasped her head with both hands, diving into the kiss, eager now.

The phone rang, jolting her in his lap and he yelped when the unexpected movement bumped his knee. She hopped off his lap. "Gabriel, I'm so sorry, I–"

"I'm fine. Answer your phone." He gritted the words, his face white beneath his tan.

Darn it. "I'm sorry." She glanced at the phone and recognized the Orange County number– the art gallery from whom she was awaiting a response. Her heartbeat galloped. At this rate, she'd be hyperventilating.

"Hi, this is Dylan." She paced toward the hall-way leading to the bedrooms, nerves propelling her.

"Hi Dylan, this is Mark O'Day from West Coast Galleries. Did I catch you at a bad time?"

Dylan forced herself to control her breathing. No need to sound like she was panting like her sister's dog Stella, eagerly awaiting a treat. Or an art exhibition, as the case may be. "Oh no, it's a great time. What can I do for you?"

"Well, I'm calling to let you know we'd love to feature the eight paintings you proposed to us. Are you still interested?"

Dylan fist pumped her phone in the air and twirled around. Cool and composed. Professional. *Ha.* "That's wonderful news. Yes, I'd be happy to work with your gallery. When were you thinking?"

"Well, another artist pulled out and so we have an immediate need."

Dylan's face fell. Was she only second choice? "Oh." So much for hiding her feelings.

"We were planning on offering you a spot in the fall, but this one opened now and I wanted to ask you first. We really like your work and you'd be doing us a favor if you were prepared sooner."

Dylan's shoulders relaxed. "So what do you mean by immediate? Next month?"

"Actually next week. Is that possible?" His voice sounded sheepish.

Dylan's jaw dropped. She'd damn well make it possible. "Of course. Did you need me to change any of the framing or…?" As she'd never had her art exhibited in a gallery, she wasn't sure what they'd need.

"I'm not sure yet. What would be great is if you could get the paintings up here, say today?"

Today? Was he kidding? Her eyes widened. She glanced over at Gabriel, who was grinning from ear to ear. Obviously he could hear the whole conversation. He nodded and gave her a thumbs up.

"I could pack them up and bring them later this afternoon." Adrenaline rushed through her veins.

"Can you bring them up yourself? Don't worry

about wrapping them up for shipping. You could just wrap them in some drop sheets. The weather and climate is the same and we've got it controlled inside the gallery. We'll help you unpack and bring them in."

Well, it wasn't like they were giving her a choice and no way would she miss out on this opportunity. "Of course. If you like, I can call you when I'm on the way up."

"That would be wonderful. We're looking forward to working with you, Dylan. We'll handle the paperwork and everything too."

Dylan shut off her phone and twirled around again. Finally!

"Bravo. My Maman already got you an exhibition?" Gabriel's grinned.

Dylan shook her head. "No, this is one of the galleries I submitted to in Laguna Beach. They said they want to do an exhibit of my work and they've got an immediate opening. Like next week."

His smiled faded for a moment. "So you got it on your own. Dylan, that's wonderful. Can I help?"

She shook her head. "These canvases are large and you've got your physical therapist coming here, right? Angela and Grant should be able to help."

He frowned. "I want to help too. And now I can see your work, non?"

She danced around the kitchen area, picking up the skillet and placing it on the large gas range.

"Sure, you can come up, but no lifting for you. Let's have some breakfast, I'll get your crutches and we'll head to my studio."

"Dylan." He held out his strong tanned hand again.

She turned, the egg carton in her hand, a spatula in the other. He was gazing at her with such warmth and pride in his eyes, that for a moment she almost forgot their engagement was fake. Maybe it was finally going to be her turn to break out. And the fact she'd gotten this show on her own, without his mother's help made it even sweeter.

"No, you're too tempting and getting the art up there today is already a nearly impossible deadline." If she went and sat on his lap again, there's no way she could resist him.

He patted his chest and pouted. "You wound me. Like I'd seduce you and keep you busy for the next few hours when you've received such exciting news? Just a little kiss?"

"We've never had just a little kiss. But we can celebrate tonight?"

His sculpted lips curved up. "We'll definitely celebrate tonight. I could come with you up to Laguna and I could take you to dinner?"

She shook her head and turned back toward the stove. "No, I need to do this one on my own, okay?" It was important to her that she walked into the gallery as an independent artist who'd garnered her first show all on her own.

He sighed. "Well, we will celebrate when you

come home."

Gabriel gritted his teeth as he crutched his way into Dylan's studio, trailing behind her dad, Angela, and her stepbrother Grant. He'd not taken one of the pain pills today, instead choosing some ibuprofen, but his leg hurt like hell and his mind struggled to tune out his injury and remain focused on his fiancée.

Sweat beaded along his upper lip and not from the exertion of hobbling through their gorgeous Mediterranean-style estate. Now Dylan had secured an exhibition on her own, what if she decided she no longer needed their fake engagement? Sure his mother's connections in the art world could greatly accelerate her career, but after his screw up yesterday, he wouldn't blame Dylan for backing out. Their bargain was unequal—at best—and he had more to gain and to lose than she did.

He needed to turn things around and act more like a partner than a hindrance. Fast. If only he could help her with the paintings or drive up to Laguna with her.

"So which paintings are you taking with you? They're all so wonderful, sweetie." Angela stood with her hand on Dylan's shoulder, a warm smile on her face.

"You're too kind." Dylan bit her lip and reached up and twisted her long silky auburn hair into a topknot, revealing her slender ivory neck. "I showed them the sunrise and sunset collection I painted last autumn, several of the sunsets from the hilly pasture with the ocean view. One has Lacy, Buttercup, and Bianca grazing with the sun setting in the background."

Gabriel approached, eager to see her work. He gazed over her shoulder and sucked in a quick breath. *Mon Dieu.* The painting facing him was a visual masterpiece.

Dylan had captured the late afternoon sky with a stunning melding of shades ranging from the palest rose to deep violet. The setting sun was a brilliant focal point, framed by the forest green trees and verdant rolling hills. Just like the Impressionist masters she emulated, she'd portrayed the play of light and shadow beautifully. But her work added other elements—a slightly more modern edge that punched up some of the colors and the texture. The piece leapt off the page. Alive.

Oh yes, she was talented. If the rest of her paintings looked like this one, she would be wildly successful. Once people saw them, she wouldn't need extra assistance.

"Dylan, this is *vraiment incroyable*. Truly incredible. My god you are talented."

"That's what we've been telling her for years." Chris said, paternal pride written on his rugged face.

She angled her head back toward him, a rosy glow suffusing her high cheekbones. "Do you really think so?" A tinge of vulnerability colored her voice.

He brushed a fiery strand of hair back from her brow and kissed her. "Absolutely. You're going to be a star."

She smiled against his mouth, and then stepped back. "We'll see."

"Wait, you've never seen her paintings before and you're engaged? How is that possible?" Grant asked, a frown slashing across his face.

"You haven't seen Dylan's work before?" Angela stared at him, her dark brows drawn together.

Zut. "I've just never seen them in person because they are all here in California." That sounded reasonable, right? It was true.

Dylan stepped back and slid her arm around him. "It's not Gabriel's fault. In Paris, there just wasn't time before I came home. And I wouldn't show them to him online. He had to wait until he got here."

Gabriel's shoulders relaxed. One question they hadn't rehearsed together on the drive down to Pacific Vista Ranch.

"Just how much time have you guys actually spent together?" Grant crossed his arms across his broad chest, suddenly looking very much like an over-protective older brother.

"Oh Grant, come on. We've spent enough time to know how we feel." Dylan's chocolate brown eyes narrowed.

"Well, your engagement was really fast." Chris cocked his head and stared at them, considering.

"Please." Gabriel held up his hands. "We understand your concerns, my parents said the exact same thing. But when you know, you just know. And with my travel schedule, well my former travel schedule, we would spend time apart anyway. Both Dylan and I are independent, but just because we Skyped more than we were physically together doesn't mean we don't love each other and know we want to be together." He reached down and interlaced his fingers with Dylan's.

She gazed up at him, gratitude shining in her dark eyes before facing her family again. "Quality over quantity, but that's all changed now." She squeezed his hand.

Nobody said anything for a moment and Gabriel searched for more words to convince her family they were truly ready to get married.

"You've always known how you feel immediately, Dylan." Angela smiled at them. "Now we need to get these paintings ready to go. I brought up all those old sheets. And Gabriel, you should have a seat over on the lounger. No work for you."

Gabriel forced a smile. Being inactive and unable to assist sucked. "Let me see the rest of the collection first. And then my physical therapist should be here in about half an hour, so I'll have to return to the guesthouse soon." He'd be damned if he reclined like an invalid and had them parade the paintings in front of him.

"I'm going to prop them up along the wall so I can label each one after we wrap it up. You can see them from the chair." Dylan was already shifting the large frames over against the broad white wall.

"And I'll give you a ride back down to the house, okay?" Angela smiled sympathetically at him.

"I appreciate it. Now let me see the rest." He beamed at Dylan. What mattered most was that this beautiful woman was about to fulfill one of her lifelong dreams.

Gabriel laid the crutches along the hardwood floor and sank onto the cushioned furniture. No way would he admit that his leg had been throbbing, but sitting felt much better. How far he'd fallen. Dylan's family was so proud and so protective of her—he couldn't help but compare how different they were from his own.

Of course, his mother was supportive of he and his sister's dreams, but their father was only worried about following the rules and maintaining traditions that no longer applied in the modern world. Would his father ever speak so glowingly about Claude running the winery or creating a new award-winning wine? If his father opened his eyes, he'd see that his daughter was the one with the passion and the talent to be at the helm of DuVernay. How incredible that Dylan's parents supported her dreams without question.

He was proud to call her his fiancée.

Even if it was just for a while.

CHAPTER 19

GABRIEL GROANED AND SANK INTO the scorching hot water in the enormous jetted bathtub. The last hour had been hell with his physical therapist. He'd thought he had a high pain tolerance, but Carolyn Browne, a former Olympic runner, took it all to a new level.

Of course he wanted to heal as fast as possible.

Of course he wanted to be back on his feet and not allow the rest of his body to atrophy. But damn, the "massage" portion of his physical therapy had felt more like he'd been peppered with a hammer and chisel. He sighed, closed his eyes, and rested his head back against the wide ceramic tub rim. The pulsating jets of water soothed and the heat was heavenly. He was more tired than he'd ever admit and right now, he'd soak in this tub as long as he could get away with it. Dylan wasn't returning from Laguna Beach for a few more hours.

His eyes flew open again and he gazed out the window. The golden rays of the afternoon sun bathed the riot of bougainvillea clustered around the wide glass frame. His fiancée certainly had

the benefit of an incredible setting for her paintings and the light here rivaled the famous light of
Provence, where many of the original Impressionists had been inspired. Although he had assumed
Dylan's talent would be impressive, nothing could
have prepared him for the raw extent of it. She
had a true gift.

His phone rang and his sister Claude's name
flashed on the screen. He disabled the video portion for obvious reasons and answered. "Bonjour."

"Gabriel. How are you?"

Gabriel rolled his eyes and was glad she couldn't
read his expression. No need to stress his sister out.
"I've just had my first physical therapy and let's
just say she could have worked in the dungeons of
the family chateau back in the day. Hopefully it
will be a fast recovery."

"Oh, I'm so sorry. I'm just so sorry this all happened. I wish I could be there with you." Concern
laced through her voice.

"There's nothing to do right now. It's more
important for you to be there, working on the
new rosé, and keeping an eye on your winery."

She snorted. "My winery. Tell Papa that. But it
is all going well and I'm confident about the new
wine. But we need to make a plan for you."

Like he wasn't already embroiled in enough
plots. "How do you mean?"

"Well the whole point of you being there with
that woman is to buy you time. Maman filled me
in on the plan and it's a great idea. But what are
you going to do? This is only temporary. Have

you thought about afterward? Your next career?"

Gabriel winced. He loved his little sister, but sometimes she pushed a little too hard, too soon. "Well, it's only been a few weeks since my life was destroyed. I don't have a plan written out in ink yet. And that woman's name is Dylan."

"I'm sorry. I know it is fast, but I'm stuck here with Papa and you know how he is. He's scheming how quickly he can make you return. I wouldn't be surprised if he was bribing your doctors to clear you to travel as soon as possible."

"Oh come on, why is he so damn eager to retire early? What is he going to do with his life any-way? He's not even sixty. He can't force me to come back." He ground his back molars together.

"I hope not. But in the meanwhile, I've been thinking."

Uh-oh. "Oui?"

"We have two issues: convincing Papa he can-not force you to run the winery, and convincing him I am capable of running the business on my own."

"True. Well, your work speaks for itself and everyone at the winery and in the industry knows it. It seems women run more wineries in France and Italy now. He just needs to open his eyes. And release his stubborn hold on this past legacy crap. It's ludicrous." He shook his head.

"Gabriel, I must tell you what I heard. You need to know. He was speaking with his attorneys and I overheard him talking about cutting you out of the will if you refuse to take your rightful place."

Her voice was hushed.

Gabriel sat up and yelped when his knee bumped the edge of the tub. Damn it, he couldn't even take a damn bath without repercussions. "Are you joking? Does Maman know about this?"

"I don't think so. She'd be furious and I think she also has to agree. My point is, he is not kidding about this."

"Well, I have more than enough money, so if he wants to do that, so be it." But Gabriel's chest tightened. It wasn't so much about the money, but more about his family's name. More about his father seeing him as his flesh and blood and not an arbitrary figurehead. Although he didn't want to run their vineyards and business, he was still a DuVernay.

"Oh, Gabriel, you know it's not about the money. I just hate to see our family be torn apart over this."

His temples began to throb, competing for attention with his screaming knee. "Well, it's him doing this. Maman agrees with you and me and it is just his pig-headed archaic beliefs causing all of us problems."

"I have an idea that might be something to appease him and ensure we all get what we want."

Gabriel blew out a breath, willing his simmering temper not to blow. "Okay?"

"Well, Maman told me the climate on your fiancée's ranch is very similar to here in our Rhone Valley and I confirmed it with some research." She paused for a few moments. "What if you took some vine clippings and started a small DuVernay production in California?"

Gabriel's jaw dropped. "What?"

"Hear me out. It's not like you hate the family business, you just don't want to be tied here and shoulder all the burden, right?"

"Right." He did love wine and viticulture–it was in his blood after all.

"So, if Papa thought you were interested in carrying on the DuVernay, non, *expanding* the DuVernay name, perhaps he'd be more open to you doing that in America and me running it here." Claude's voice rose.

Gabriel scratched his jaw and returned his gaze out to the gorgeous Pacific Vista Ranch scenery. Claude was correct–he'd even seen some vines growing when they'd driven to Dylan's home. The soil here was probably excellent, at least for some of the grapes the DuVernay's were famous for. The climate was similar, although the proximity to the ocean could be an issue.

"You make a good point. But what happens when Dylan and I end this engagement? I won't be living here anymore. This plan, too, is only temporary." His chest tightened.

"What if your engagement doesn't end?"

Gabriel froze and tamped down a hint of alarm tickling his throat. "Claude, right now I cannot think that far ahead. We've got a business arrangement with, um, benefits. I don't know if I could ask her for more. She's already giving me so much."

"Maman said you two really have feelings for each other. Do you?" His baby sister's voice grew teasing.

Gabriel paused. "Well, I've never felt this way about another woman, but that's not a big surprise. She is different."

Claude pounced. "See? You do love her."

"Love? Please. Being so close to Papa is making you a little dramatic. Look, I'll think about it. But right now, I've got to focus all my attention on my recovery and on fulfilling my side of the bargain for Dylan. She's got a show next week and I want to be in shape to go and support her." Their engagement couldn't end yet.

"Maman already got her an exhibition? Wow, that was fast. Is she any good?"

"No, she got this show on her own. She's got a singular talent. So see? Already another point of me needing her much more than she needs me. Not really the time for me to ask about plowing up her family's ranch and planting vines." His shoulders slumped at the truth of his words.

"See, you love her. Otherwise why would you care? But you should think about the vines." She paused for a few moments. "I mean, what does your manager say about the football world for you? Are there opportunities there?"

Gabriel blew out a noisy exhale. "Perhaps. There's commentating. Possibly coaching."

"Oh, you'd be incredible in both. Couldn't you do it all? Grow vines, and the football?"

His lips twitched, despite the gravity of their

discussion. "You are stubborn as a mule. It's a wonder you haven't convinced Papa to give you the winery."

Claude laughed. "One day he will. But please think about my suggestions. I've got to run. I love you."

"Love you too, brat." Gabriel powered off the phone and set it back on the marble tile surrounding the luxurious tub.

He slid forward in the bath and submerged his head under the water. His mind was spinning. Not just with the suggestions and ideas his sister presented about the winery, but her observations about Dylan.

Love?

What did he know about love? Aside from the loyalty and caring he felt for his mother and little sister, he'd never experienced true romantic love. There'd never been time, nor frankly any desire to focus on anything but football. His sport had been his mistress and realizing that wasn't going to be the case any longer wouldn't be an overnight adjustment. He liked Dylan. He admired her and was insanely attracted to her. But love wasn't something he knew anything about.

A loud scream drew him spluttering up from beneath the surface. Dylan was bending over the tub, her eyes wide and wild. "What are you doing? Why would you be underwater?"

For a second, Gabriel simply stared, not comprehending her distress. He wiped the water away from his eyes and said, "Hello?"

Her breath whooshed out and she sank down onto the broad rim of the tub. "Oh my god, I was calling your name and you didn't answer. When I came in here, your phone was sitting here and you were nowhere to be seen. I walked over and you were under the water. I thought–"

He reached for her hand. "Oh, Dylan, you couldn't have thought–" His lips twitched.

"It isn't funny." Color rose in her cheeks, she tugged her hand free, and stalked across the room. She leaned against the vanity, sparking his memory of the other night when they'd had a very interesting time against that piece of furniture.

He forced his attention back to the present. "Ma chérie, I would never harm myself. I'm sorry to scare you. But you must know me well enough by now to know that."

She crossed her arms and glared. "What? Because we've slept together and compared notes about our lives, I should know you well enough? All I know is you've been devastated, understandably so, you've lost your career, you may never run again, and you've entered into a fake engagement to avoid your father. So, no. I don't know what you might do."

Gabriel's heart warmed in an unfamiliar way. He reached out his hand again. "Please forgive me? The water just feels really good and I've got a lot on my mind. Join me." His cock leapt to attention under the water–the idea of her tight little body sliding into the tub with him tempting as hell.

Her pink lips parted. "Join you?"

"The water's warm and you've been working all day. Join me in the tub and tell me about the gallery and the exhibit. I want to hear all about it." And he did want to hear all about it. After he got her naked in the tub.

"Well, when you put it that way..." Her mouth curved up into a teasing grin and in one swift movement, she whipped the navy and white striped t-shirt over her head, revealing her small perfect breasts.

Suddenly, the bathwater chilled because he was on fire. "Please."

"Please what? Oh, tell you about today? The gallery is gorgeous and they're giving me a prime spot–" Her hands paused at the waistband of her faded denim capris.

"Dylan." He cursed his bum knee and gripped the edges of the tub. "Don't make me come get you."

She giggled. "I'm coming. Don't hurt yourself. Just be patient." She remained right out of reach.

He bared his teeth at her. Oh, once he got her in the tub with him, she'd pay for torturing him this way.

Driving him completely insane, she slowly peeled off her jeans, inch-by-inch. Her creamy skin was flushed pink, and was offset by the tiniest black thong he'd ever seen. She looped her fingers in the edges of her panties, not taking her eyes from his. Her breath came in short bursts, revealing she was just as excited as he was.

"These too?" She bit her plump lower lip and held her ground.

He narrowed his gaze. "Please chérie, you're killing me."

She considered him for an interminable moment, her eyes hooded and her full lips curved up, pure seductress, absolute goddess. She slid the panties off and stood before him in all her stunning beauty. If he didn't get to touch her soon, he'd explode.

Knee be damned, he would come get her. It would be worth the sacrifice. He started to rise from the tub.

She crossed the few steps to the bath, lifted one toned leg and dipped a dainty hot pink toe into the water.

He snaked his hand out and caught her slender ankle. "No more teasing. Now." He bit the words out, desperate for her.

With a feline smile, she entered the bath, carefully straddling him and slowly sinking down until she was on her knees. She perched on his thighs and reached under the water and wrapped her strong artistic fingers around him. "Is this still teasing?"

He groaned, his back arching as she stroked her thumb around his tip. "Oh my god Dylan. I need you."

He gripped her sweet hips and lifted her. She released him and braced her hands on his shoulders. "Now Gabriel, now."

He lowered her down until he'd filled her completely and slid his hands around to grip her trim heart-shaped ass. Her wet heat clamped around him and he almost exploded inside her. She started to move, but he held her still.

"Give me a second or that's all I'll have for you." He gritted the words.

She wove her arms up around his neck and leaned in and kissed him, her breath sweet and hot. He moved one hand up to grasp the back of her slender ivory neck and stroked his tongue against hers. She began to ride him, slowly at first, rising up and sliding back down. He clasped her waist and encouraged her lead, while supporting her weight.

The water sloshed along the edges of the tub and she increased her pace, rocking herself against him. She shifted back and reached her arms up and caressed her breasts, tugging at her taut pink nipples, her breath coming in pants now.

Gabriel's lower spine began to tingle and burn. He shifted one hand back to her gently curved hip and stroked her where they were joined with the other, spurring her on. She cried his name and fell forward against him, tremors starting inside her, gripping him with the pulsations. The feel of her undulating on him was enough to send him over the edge. He pressed her hips down on him and exploded inside her.

For a moment, their mingled breath was the only sound in the room. Dylan turned her head slightly and pressed an open-mouthed kiss against his throat and Gabriel hugged her in closer.

Couldn't get her close enough.

She lifted her head and stared at him, her enormous dark eyes heavy-lidded, her lips swollen and red. "Wow."

He threw back his head and laughed. "Wow is right."

She laughed with him, joy filling her face now. "I'm starving. I stopped by the main house and Angela had made us plates of her fettuccine Bolognese, salad, and garlic bread. Sound good?"

His heart skipped a beat in his chest. Her radiance and passion warmed him from the inside out. Every moment together with her was incredible, and not just the lovemaking. How would he ever be able to leave her?

Dylan curled her legs underneath her on the dining room chair and forked in another bite of delicious fettuccine. She was famished after the long but exhilarating day. She glanced up and caught Gabriel's eyes closed in pleasure as he swallowed.

"Pretty amazing, right?"

He nodded and grinned. Why would you ever cook yourself if Angela is this talented in the kitchen. Does she always make enough for take-away?"

She laughed. "My sisters and I say the same thing. Angela loves to cook and the more the merrier. We're lucky."

He reached one strong hand over and gently

cupped her chin, gazed into her eyes and said, "I'm the lucky one."

Color rose in her cheeks. What had gotten into her doing that slow striptease while he watched from the bathtub? Not that she was shy, she was comfortable with her sensuality and her body, but she'd gotten more aroused watching him watching her than she could have imagined. "We're both lucky. Let's leave it at that." She dropped her gaze to her plate, finding it easier to focus on food than the gleam in his emerald green eyes.

He dropped his hand. "So, tell me about the gallery. Are you pleased?" His gaze remained intent, signaling his true interest in her response.

She sat up straighter in the chair. "I'm ecstatic actually. The gallery is small, but prestigious, right on the main drag in Laguna Beach. My work will be up in the front half of the gallery, with a few paintings visible in the front window."

"That's super. And the paperwork?"

"All good. We made a few minor tweaks to the pricing I suggested, even increasing it on a few pieces. Standard commissions and such. This collection will be in the gallery for three months."

"But what if all the paintings are purchased right away? At the show?" His winged brows rose.

She snorted. "Highly doubtful."

"You never know. Maybe I want them." He swirled the pasta around the tines of his fork and took another bite.

"Don't you dare." She shook her head.

"But they are incredible. Why can't I buy them

if I want them?" His handsome brow furrowed.

"Because I want strangers to see my art and buy it. Not my friends and family doing it to support me." She placed her fork onto the edge of her plate.

He nodded, his eyes serious now. "I understand what you are saying, but you also must understand we've not known each other very long and from that perspective, I fell for your paintings when I first saw them. Not because of our connection, but because I connected to the beauty."

Her heart performed a slow roll in her chest. How did he always say the right thing? His irresistible charm and sincerity threatened the tenuous boundaries she'd tried to erect. Distance, she needed more than arms distance between them for a minute.

She grabbed her wineglass, popped to her feet, and headed to the refrigerator. "Would you like a little more wine?"

"I'm trying to limit myself to one glass for a while longer, but thank you."

She took her time topping off her glass, gathering her composure around her like the edges of her favorite silk shawl. Business arrangement. Fake engagement.

This. Would. End.

She rejoined him at the table, her invisible defensive cloak in place. "Anyway, the show is next Thursday night. Will you feel up for it do you think?"

He winced and nodded. "Oui. The physical therapist insists the sooner she has me on my feet the better. Either way, even if I have to lean against the wall or my crutches, I wouldn't miss your first show for anything."

Her shoulders softened. "Was she that bad?"

He threw up his hands. "The toughest. She almost had me crying like a baby. But if it is effective, I can handle it."

"Anything else exciting happen today?" Keep the conversation normal. Regular. Light.

He shook his head. "I have a call tomorrow with my manager to discuss some opportunities. We'll see."

"Are these jobs here in the States? What you're hoping for?"

He shrugged. "We shall see. I've got time on my visa and it will be a while until I'm mobile enough to do anything." He paused and stared down at his plate.

Darn it, she hated seeing him in pain. She walked over to him and ran her hands around the back of his neck. His muscles were bunched and knotted beneath his silky smooth skin, so she began to massage the tight cords to help him relax.

"Mmm…that feels incredible. You are too good to me." He stretched under her hands like a cat being petted.

She leaned down and kissed his cheek. "It's been a long day, why don't we go to bed."

He reached back and clasped her hand and tugged her around so she landed on his lap, again just narrowly missing his knee. He slid his hands up and tilted her chin up to meet his kiss. "I thought you'd never ask."

CHAPTER 20

DYLAN STRODE ALONG THE SOFT green grass, the soles of her riding boots silent. Her phone vibrated in the pocket of her worn jeans as she headed to meet her sisters for a quick ride. She'd been in the studio since 7 a.m. and needed a break, especially after her very long day yesterday and even longer night with Gabriel.

Although every sensual second last night was worth her bleary eyes and sore muscles today.

She fished the phone out and glanced at the display.

I miss you already.

Her heartbeat kicked up. *Miss you too. I'll be back after my ride.*

She smiled at the phone. Living with him definitely wasn't a hardship so far.

Breeding season was winding down, so her sisters had time for a midday break. Sam and Amanda weren't just her siblings; they were also her best friends. Lying to them directly was rough. She'd managed to dodge too many questions about Gabriel, but this ride could turn into an interrogation. Especially with her twin.

She paused for a moment before she crested the hill leading into the barn. Time to compose herself and fortify her defenses. Hiding her emotions wasn't exactly one of her top skills. Or even bottom ones. Well, she was sexually satisfied and wouldn't that quality show up as evidence of being in love?

"There you are. Come on, Dylan, I've already got Lacy saddled. We've only got an hour. Chop chop." Sam bellowed from the depths of the barn.

Ah, her twin sister–the picture of patience. She snorted.

"I'm right here. No need to yell..." She stepped into the spacious barn. Pacific Vista Ranch boasted several large stables, and this smaller twenty-one-horse barn was for the family's horses and the resident stallion, Hercules. Glimmers of sunshine bathed the space with a golden glow and dust motes sparkled in the breeze. Quiet whinnies of the remaining horses filled the air. The comforting scents of hay and horse soothed the anxiety humming through her system.

Sam was already leading her beautiful bay, Lacy, outside to join Buttercup and Bianca, her sisters' horses. Amanda was already her mare on the other side of the open-ended entrance.

Although she didn't work with the animals like her sister Sam did as breeding manager and Amanda in her role as the resident equine vet, she loved them just as much. In fact, she'd discovered her love of drawing and painting when she started painting them after moving to the ranch. She'd found consolation in her art and she had several portraits of the resident ranch horses. Which was about one hundred and twenty at this point.

Riding and soaking up the beauty of the ranch always soothed her. Something the entire McNeill clan had in common. Their ranch sprawled over more than two hundred acres of lush greenery and colorful flowers and plants. After her mostly sleepless night and her jangled nerves surrounding her anticipation of questions about Gabriel, a brisk ride with her sisters and some fresh air would help balance out the stress. Hopefully.

She hurried through, murmuring words to the horses that poked their heads out of their stalls. She joined her sisters and climbed up onto her sweet mare with four white socks and white blaze on her forehead. Instead of heading out onto the Rancho Santa Fe riding trails, which ran along-side the local roads and ranch estates, they'd decided to ride around their property. She wasn't in the mood to wave and make small talk with their neighbors.

They trotted off together and the early summer sunshine warmed her face. Lacy's solid strength beneath her bolstered her spirits and reminded her to stay present.

Her sisters chattered about the upcoming plans for Amanda and Jake's wedding. They'd chosen a small celebration with family and close friends at the ranch. Holt and Sam had been married back in February on one of the gorgeous bluffs on the sprawling property. Holt was perfect for Sam and they were blissfully happy. Jake was the ideal guy for her quieter sister Amanda and the two of them, although almost total opposites, balanced each other in ways nobody could have predicted. She was thrilled for them.

Both her sisters had been sheltered, mostly by their own choice to stay close to the ranch and avoid casual dating. Both their careers were thriving when they'd met their guys.

Until Dylan achieved her own professional goals, she hadn't wanted to muddy the waters with a serious relationship. Up until meeting Gabriel, she'd been happy to date around and didn't feel as tethered to the ranch as her sisters.

Ever since her sisters had fallen in love with their forever guys, they'd wanted Dylan to do the same. Amanda had tried to set Dylan up with any number of Jake's firefighter co-workers and Sam pestered her to get out more. While she appreciated their intentions, she didn't need a matchmaker.

"Earth to Dylan. I asked you how yesterday went at the gallery?" Amanda asked.

"Sorry, I just haven't ridden in a few weeks and I'm soaking it in. Everything went great. The show's next Thursday night and my paintings will be in the front of the gallery for the next three months."

"That's great." Sam added.

Dylan beamed. *Yes it was.* "You both can come, right?"

"Of course. We're all coming. Will Gabriel be

up for it?" Sam's tone sharpened.

Uh-oh. "He's going to make it work, even if we have to sit him in a chair for the evening." Would he have come to her show if he hadn't been injured and they were just dating?

Amanda cleared her throat. "Dylan, can I ask you a question?"

Somehow her sisters had flanked her, were crowding her. Here it came. "Sure."

"We're a little concerned that you dove into this engagement really quickly. Are you sure you're ready for marriage?" Amanda's calm voice asked from her left.

Dylan took a deep breath and held it, counting to three.

"It's just we've seen the stories on him. He's never had a serious girlfriend; he's been photographed with other women over the last year when you guys were supposedly together. What if he's using you?" Sam's voice was urgent on her right side.

They are just being protective. Too protective. Dylan inhaled a deep breath and released it slowly. "Using me for what? Look, you know I love you both more than anything." She looked at each of her sisters in turn.

"You both know how the paparazzi are—he's a gorgeous, popular athlete. Fans approach him all the time for pictures and sure, he took a few different women to events where he needed a plus one. I knew about it and it's not a big deal. I trust him completely. Don't you trust me?"

Dylan hated lying to her sisters more than she hated turning the tables on them. Now, she was so deep in the web of deception, if she confessed, they'd think she was more naïve and impulsive than they already did. She didn't need a lecture about taking off the rose-colored glasses her family assumed she wore 24/7. Besides, she'd promised Gabriel to keep their deal confidential.

"Oh sweetie, that's not what we're saying. It's just…" Amanda paused and cleared her throat again. "It's just you're such a romantic. I can't speak for Sam, but I'm a little hurt you didn't confide in me. You moped over him when you got back from Paris. You used to have a different guy every month and that almost stopped. I just don't know why you'd be so secretive."

Dylan's shoulders stiffened and she gazed off toward the horizon. "It's just..." To her horror, tears rose in her eyes and she blinked furiously to prevent them from spilling out from beneath her dark sunglasses.

"Dylan, if something is going on, please tell us. I hate that you felt you couldn't talk about falling in love with me. I know I'm selfish as hell and was wrapped up in Holt, but are you sure? I'd hate for you to be jumping into this because of his charm or you feel like you need to be married too or—"

"Seriously Sam? Yes, you guessed it. I hated being the single sister so much I figured I'd marry the first guy who asked. Give me some credit, please." Dylan didn't bother to temper the sarcasm. She pulled gently on Lacy's reins, and halted. "I'm heading back."

"Wait. Please. I'm sorry. I guess my feelings are hurt too. I know you're impulsive and I love you and just don't want you to get hurt, okay? Don't be mad." Sam pleaded.

"Please don't be upset." Amanda echoed.

"Give me a little while to cool off. I'll be fine, but I wish you would trust that I'm grown up enough to make my own decisions?" The guilt gnawed at her. Her sisters could *never* find out she'd lied to them and her relationship wasn't real.

The break-up would have to be spectacular. Honestly, she hadn't really thought that part through when she'd agreed to his mother's scheme. Actually, she hadn't really thought most of it through. Six months had seemed like a lifetime away, but less than one month in and her feelings deepened for Gabriel every day. His sweet supportiveness and their mind-blowing chemistry were a potent combination. Maybe her sisters had valid reasons to be concerned.

"Of course. I'm sorry. You know I'm over-protective. I can't help it. And Gabriel seems like a lovely guy. If you love him, we'll trust your judgment. We could even start discussing your wedding. Will you guys have it on the ranch too?" Amanda, always the peacemaker in the family soothed.

"Can we just finish our ride? No wedding plans yet. We wanted to be engaged, but we plan on a long engagement because we're perfectly aware most of our relationship has been long distance.

So let's stick to yours, Amanda. Did you decide on October?" Dylan stuffed the realization she was falling for Gabriel away for now.

Amanda nodded. "We can talk about it later. Let's enjoy this gorgeous day." They cantered along and for a few blessed minutes, the beat of hooves along the rolling green hills, and the chirping of a flock of small birds flying nearby.

"Oh, I did want to share with you both that I spoke to Grant and he's staying indefinitely." Amanda said.

"For good? And when is Callie joining him?" Dylan asked. Callie was Grant's Australian wife. Before meeting his wife, he'd been a nomad, traveling the world. She was from Melbourne and they'd settled there.

Amanda frowned. "Grant didn't say. I think they might be having issues."

"Are they still trying to get pregnant?" Sam asked. They'd been married three years.

"He just said things were strained right now and he had some decisions to make. You know he can be guarded. Hopefully, everything was okay and Callie just couldn't get away because of work." Amanda's voice was tinged with concern.

Dylan frowned. "Well, they've already suffered three miscarriages. I mean, she didn't come for Sam and Holt's wedding in February because she'd been afraid to fly. And if she were pregnant right now, I doubt Grant would be here, right?"

Sam's brow creased. "I hope they can figure it out. He seemed so happy with her."

"Well, life can be unpredictable, you know?" Dylan said. Gabriel's life was on a different trajectory now and who knew where he'd end up.

"Race you back to the house." Sam dug her heels into Princess Buttercup and flew off in front.

Amanda and Dylan whooped and galloped to pass their sister. The brilliant green fields dotted with horses grazing on the pastures as far as the eye could see zoomed by. With the wind whipping across her face and hair, the warmth of the perfect seventy-degree day warming her, exhilaration filled Dylan—just the respite she'd been seeking.

There was plenty of time to worry about Gabriel later.

CHAPTER 21

GABRIEL PLACED THE GLASS OF water on the stone patio table and sank into the lime green cushions. He wrapped the ice pack around his knee and elevated it on one of the white and navy striped throw pillows. Once he was comfortable, he double-checked his phone. Just in the nick of time.

In two minutes he had a Facetime call with his agent. Being idle didn't sit well with him–time to focus on what he could do besides just rehabbing his knee and pretending he was getting married. He closed his eyes for a moment, allowing the soft summer breeze to soothe his skin and inhaled the sweet fragrance of the clusters of crimson flowers that framed the guesthouse's private back patio.

Calm and reasonable–he'd be professional–no matter what Bernard shared with him today.

His phone rang and Bernard's lean, wolfish face was there on video. "Allo."

"Where are you? The magic garden?" Bernard asked.

"The back patio. Tell me the news." He rubbed the tense muscles on the back of his neck.

"I think you'll be pleased. Have you spoken to Davis yet?"

Gabriel shook his head. "Non. Did you speak with him?"

"Oui. So, you have some excellent options. Remember I mentioned the option of being a television commentator?"

Gabriel sat up straighter in the chair "Perhaps. What does it entail?"

"Well all the big sports channels and the major networks would love to have you. They find you 'charming' and your English 'excellent.'" Bernard snickered.

Gabriel bared his teeth. "Oh so they just want me to be charming and that's it? Anything about my expertise? My observation skills? My damn record?" Being the best had driven his entire life. While he'd been born with natural athletic talent, he prided himself on being the first one to practice and the last one to leave, especially once he'd started being singled out for his success.

"Expertise? Who needs that when you're so pretty and look so good in underwear billboard ads?" Bernard was cracking himself up.

"Screw you, LeVeque. Don't be bitter because you have a face like a sheep. I can hire a new manager anytime. Maybe an American. Want to call me back when you're ready to be serious?" Sometimes he wondered why he still employed Bernard and if anybody found the man amusing.

"Whoa. No need to get upset. You've got to keep your sense of humor." His agent held up his hands. "Of course they know you're the best in the world. They've written pages and pages and waxed poetic about your work ethic. I'm just yanking your chain."

Gabriel shrugged a shoulder. "So be serious and tell me the offers."

"Well, the best one in my opinion is from ESPN. They share your vision of elevating soccer in America to one of the top sports, up there with football, baseball, and basketball. All the kids in this country are playing soccer more and more. The timing is excellent. You've got clout. A U.S. team gave you the biggest deal in history—all of that factors in."

Gabriel's shoulders softened. "I thought I'd make my mark playing..." He exhaled an unsteady breath. "But this could be an option."

"You have made your mark and you can make a big impact this way. So, they'd love to set up a meeting with you and discuss timing and contracts and such. When do you think you'd be up for going up to L.A.? I could send a car for you."

"Let's give it a week or two, okay? I'd like to be done with these damn crutches first. And Dylan's got a gallery show next week and I won't risk being late like I was to the engagement party." No way would he disappoint her again.

"We don't want to wait too long. And before I tell you about what the Galaxy is offering, how long do you plan on keeping up this engagement? All these opportunities I'm bringing to you will ensure your status in the country so you don't need to get married for a green card."

Gabriel jolted and slammed down his glass on the table, liquid splashing everywhere. "I'm not marrying her for a green card. What the hell?"

Bernard threw up his hands. "Oh come on, Gabriel. I've known you for what, ten years now? Marriage? Please. No need for a charade."

"It's not a charade, damn you." They were a real couple. They would have been a real couple if he hadn't gotten injured. He'd sought her out once he arrived in California because he'd never gotten her completely off his mind. Granted, they'd probably be enjoying a long distance, casual relationship, but his attraction to her wasn't feigned.

"So you are in love with her. Want to be father to her children. Have a wedding date planned?" Bernard was shaking his head now.

Love.

Why did everyone keep throwing the "L" word around? "Look. Dylan and I met last summer in Paris. She is special to me. Now, this is a business discussion. If you want to continue having business discussions with me as your client, I suggest you shut your mouth, refrain from making any more insinuations to me or anyone else, and tell me about the Galaxy. *Comprends*?"

Bernard's small mouth hung open for a moment, then snapped shut. "I apologize. I will not bring it up again." He paused and looked down at some notes on his desk.

"So now the other option or perhaps combination of options is as an assistant coach with the

Galaxy. Obviously, the salary would be very different than your player package. Do you wish to pursue discussions on this front?"

Gabriel forced himself to focus on business, although if Bernard were sitting outside on this paradise-like patio with him, he would have throttled him. "Coaching has always been something in the back of my mind, but something I thought would come much later in life."

"And now?"

Gabriel shook his head. "It's too soon for me. I need some space from my own playing." Needed more time before he could share all his knowledge and skills with athletes who would score the goals and receive the glory. It would have been one thing to triumphantly retire from the game at the appropriate time and then coach. But now? Gabriel couldn't envision it.

Maybe in a few years the sting of having his dreams ripped out from under him would fade. He'd have to get over the devastation one day, but that day was not today.

"I agree and I believe Davis figured it was a long shot." Bernard clapped his hands together. "I will set up a meeting for us in two to three weeks. Will that be long enough?"

"Perfect."

"Gabriel, I sincerely apologize about what I said about Dylan." His agent's voice was sincere.

"Okay. I know it was all very fast. If anyone says anything to you on this front, you make sure no rumors arise, got it? You may share that Dylan and I met last summer." He'd protect Dylan and her family with everything in his power.

"Of course. I'll be in touch." The screen went dark.

Gabriel set down the phone and leaned his head back on the comfortable cushioned chair. Did Dylan's family or the team believe he was engaged to Dylan to stay in the country? On some level, yes he was with her to stay in the country and avoid his father, but he could get his own visa without marrying for citizenship.

Damn, this clever strategy of his mother's became more complex each passing day.

Dylan strolled through the guesthouse to the open French doors. Gabriel appeared to be snoozing on one of the lounge chairs. She tiptoed closer and gazed down at his handsome features. She'd love to paint him like this, with his sculpted mouth parted and his dark lashes forming a crescent along the top of his chiseled cheekbones–she'd call it Adonis at rest. Smiling at her silliness, unable to resist, she bent down and brushed her lips against his.

His hand flew up and clasped the back of her head and the next thing she knew, she was landing in his lap. Again. He deepened the kiss, parting her lips, and delving inside. His breath was cool and minty and delicious. She wrapped her arms around his neck.

"Mmm...I could wake up like this every day."

He murmured against her lips. He shifted her hips so she was fully on his lap, his impressive erection pressing against her.

She laughed and leaned back. "You were just pretending to sleep, looking all innocent, to lure me in. I know your tricks."

"Caught me. I heard you coming and figured if I could play possum, I'd catch you. Now I've got you." He smiled and hugged her in tight.

"How did your call go?" She had work back in her studio this afternoon, but spending a few minutes with her fiancé was reasonable. Knowing their volatile chemistry, she tried to direct the discussion to business.

"Good. Bernard is setting up some meetings in a few weeks. I may be working as a sports commentator." He nibbled along her collarbone, his breath warming her skin.

Dylan grinned even as chills shot down her body. "That's fantastic. You'll be amazing. And you'll do exactly what you've wanted to do: help bring soccer up to the next level of popularity in this country. And you'll be so good on film. All the women will want to watch."

Gabriel frowned. "Hey, I want everyone to watch because what I know about my sport."

She laughed and tapped a finger on his slightly crooked nose. "Look, I grew up in a show business family. Like it or not, it matters what you look like on screen. Don't be offended. I know you're more than just a pretty face."

He tickled her sides and growled. "How about I

show you how much more I am?"

She squirmed and squealed with laughter. "Don't tickle me. I can't take it.

"But you can take me and right now I want to take you." He slid his hands up the sides of her ribcage and cupped her breasts, rubbing his thumbs over her nipples.

Goosebumps erupted on her skin and her heat shot straight down from her taut nipples to her core. She tried to get up, but he held her in place. "I've got to be back in the studio in twenty minutes…"

He lightly bit the shell of her ear and a tremor shook her. "We have time for a, what do you call it, a speedy?"

She laughed despite her the excitement rushing through her veins. "You mean a quickie?"

"Quickie, speedy–no matter. Please, can I have you now?" His hands were everywhere, one tugging at her belt buckle, the other releasing her hair from her topknot.

She tugged his hands. "Let me up for a moment." She quickly rose and peeled off her jeans.

He shoved down the elastic waistband athletic shorts and his erection sprang free. He grasped himself in one large tanned hand. "Come back, Dylan, I've got something just for you."

She was ready and eager and willing. She climbed onto the chair, using his firm shoulders to support her. "We're making a habit of me riding you these days."

His green eyes were hooded and his jaw

clenched. "This is a habit I approve of–you're my gorgeous cowgirl." His hands framed her hips and together, they lowered her on top of him, inch by inch.

She relished the exquisite fullness. She moaned and wiggled her hips, settling in as tight as she could. Every nerve ending in her body converged right at her center, setting her aflame.

"Gabriel, I–" She was already so close to losing control.

"Ride me faster. We've only got sixteen minutes now." He urged, his voice raspy, his hands tangling in her hair that now formed a curtain around them.

Not needing any more encouragement, she gripped him with her thighs and began to move. A fine sheen of sweat covered their skin and she forgot where she ended and he began. All that remained was their passion, their connection, their lovemaking. She dug her fingers into his hair, threw back her head and cried out her release.

"Dylan." He came with her, and then wrapped his arms around her, gathering her in close.

Dylan couldn't move. Couldn't catch her breath. She turned her head and flicked her tongue along his silky bronzed skin, savoring his salty taste. Delicious. Dangerous.

Every time they made love, another sliver of her heart softened. Opened up to him. Nothing pretend with their connection.

Which was dangerous for her priorities and her life. She forced herself to pull back and ease herself off of his lap. "Let me grab a towel, I'll be right back." She hurried toward the bathroom where she grabbed her short silky red robe and dampened a washcloth.

He remained sprawled on the chair, eyes closed and lips curved up in satisfaction. Like a panther who'd just conquered and feasted and was ready to snooze. But just like the great predators, she knew he could pounce at any second.

"I've brought you a towel. I hate to be so speedy," She attempted to inject some humor in to hide the emotion simmering close to the surface. "But I've really got to get up to my studio."

"Just use and abuse me. I get it." His eyes opened and his smile deepened, the sun lines around his eyes crinkling. He reached for the towel and unselfconsciously stroked it along his ridged six-pack abs, carved hip grooves, and his lap before pulling up his shorts. "I'll be here waiting for you."

Dylan stared at him for a moment. How had this magnificent creature ended up here with her? Every moment she spent with him drew them closer together. How would it end? She shook her head out of the spell he wove around her without any effort. Just by being him.

His phone buzzed, effectively snapping her attention back, and she picked it up and handed it to him. His mother's name flashed across the screen.

He shifted in the chair and accepted the phone, glancing down and frowning.

"Bad news?" No way was she leaving prior to finding out what caused his displeasure.

He hesitated and looked up at her, his eyes wide. "My parents are coming to see me—well, see us—next week. She wants to be at your show and believes it will help her parlay your work moving forward. My papa wants to meet his future daughter-in-law."

Dylan's belly tightened. Oh crap. "Your father?"

Gabriel tossed the phone back onto the table and reached for her hand. "Yes, and I'm not excited about seeing him. He'll try to push the envelope about my returning sooner than later. We'll have to be very convincing. And she's asking if there's room for them to stay here or should they book a hotel in Laguna."

Electricity jolted from her hand through her entire body from where they were connected. Not like there wasn't already enough pressure from her first official show, convincing her own family and friends, and now a hostile fake-father-in-law-to-be. At Pacific Vista Ranch?

She leaned and pressed a quick kiss on his lips. "I'm sure my parents will insist they stay here, but I hope they choose the hotel, no offense. But we'll make sure they are up at the main house. Not here with us. No pressure. We can do it. For now I must go. I'll see you tonight."

If only she felt as confident as she sounded.

CHAPTER 22

A LTHOUGH DYLAN APPRECIATED HER
DAD treating them to a stretch limousine so
the whole family, including Gabriel's parents who
had arrived yesterday, could ride together to her
first ever gallery show, her nerves were strung
tight as a bow. If only she could have driven up
to the gallery alone and gathered her composure.
She practiced her extended exhales, inhaling for
a count of four and exhaling for a count of eight.
The breathing technique had saved her numerous
times when she felt her emotions rising faster than
she could control.

Like now.

Her first show.

She'd donned one of her favorite dresses this
evening, a slip of forest green silk, with a sharp
V neckline and asymmetrical hem. Somehow
Gabriel had managed to sit on the side with the
shorter part of the skirt, his strong hand resting on
her bare thigh. Her hair was parted in the middle and sleek down her back and her make-up
was polished and dramatic. She wasn't sure if she
looked like a famous artist, but she felt confident

in her appearance at least.

She'd assumed it would be an intimate event, with only her family and some close friends attending. Some of her art school friends who were still in Southern California were coming too. But the gallery told her it was going to be a packed house and now her imposter syndrome was kicking in. What if her family and friends had been supporting her simply because they loved her? Why the heck had she chosen to do her own interpretation of impressionism a century after Monet, Manet, Cassatt, and the rest had created masterpiece after masterpiece? She dug her fingernails into the palms of her hands, struggling to compose herself.

Michele caught her eye. "So Dylan, I know you're nervous, but this is an excellent gallery and an excellent start to your professional career. We are very excited for you." She smiled, perfect in her icy blonde beauty across the aisle.

"Merci, you are too kind. I am excited and nervous, but having Gabriel here with me, as well as my family, helps." She squeezed Gabriel's hand.

Gabriel lifted their joined hands to his lips and kissed her fingers. "I predict all her paintings sell tonight. My fiancée is very talented."

As expected, Gabriel's father was stern, cold, and bordering on rude. At least to her. He'd been perfectly charming to her parents, but every time she'd looked up over the last day, he was studying her like a butterfly pinned to a display board. Not exactly a welcoming new father-in-law.

Mr. DuVernay nodded, a speculative look on

his handsome face. Gabriel resembled his father, except his face was filled with warmth and life. "That would be excellent. I'm also happy to see you well enough to attend the show already. Your knee is improving at an excellent rate. You should be able to come home soon, non?"

Dylan jolted, but stayed still when Gabriel's fingers tightened on her leg.

Frost seeped into Gabriel's voice. "Our life is here right now. This evening belongs to Dylan and I appreciate it if you respect that."

"Well, Dylan is to be part of our family, non? She must know of your duties and expectations and that you cannot stay in America forever." His dad's hawk like gaze shifted to her. It was like he knew. Like he was searching for a chink in her armor and in the relationship. Like he was ready to jab the sword and sever their connection at the earliest opportunity.

"Didier. Enough. We're here to celebrate Dylan and get to know the McNeills." Michele gripped her husband's arm through his navy suit jacket and turned toward Sam, who was sitting with Holt on the other side of Dylan. "So Samantha, tell us about how you and Holt met."

Sam grinned. "Well, we didn't exactly get along when we first met. We met last summer when Holt came down to work as lead stuntman on a movie being filmed on our ranch. He was a real pain in the butt at first, but then I got used to having him around." Sam leaned over and kissed her husband.

Holt's appearance at Pacific Vista Ranch last year had been the catalyst to change all of the McNeills' lives forever, but so far the transformation had helped them all stop living in a bubble and expand their horizons.

Holt wrapped his arm around Sam and pulled her in closer to his side. "Let's just say Gabriel is a lucky guy to have the sweet twin. I've taken on a challenge, but she's worth every moment." His grin belied his teasing.

"I propose a toast." Chris McNeill called from the other end of the limousine. "Glasses everyone. Tonight is about celebrating our gifted artist, Dylan, who is making us all so proud with the first of many shows. Sweetheart, I've got no doubt you have a brilliant career ahead of you and also a happy lifetime with Gabriel. So, congratulations, Dylan, and welcome to the family, Gabriel."

Everyone clinked glasses, but out of the corner of her eye, Dylan caught Didier's mouth flattening in displeasure an instant prior to him sipping his champagne. She wasn't sure if he bought their relationship or not, but it was apparent that he didn't believe they needed to live in the U.S.

And the more Dylan thought about it, he was right, at least where she was concerned. Of course she wanted to be close to her family—they'd always been close—but she didn't need to work on the ranch or even live there like her sisters did.

But no, he was more interested in getting Gabriel back. And although the marriage sham was a layer of protection for Gabriel, now she could see how it wasn't foolproof. Not even close. When would Gabriel tell his father he'd be staying here, working as a sports commentator? Then, he would be able to end their pretend relationship, eliminating any chance of it becoming real. Her stomach dropped.

"Dylan." Gabriel reached up and smoothed the line forming between her brows. He leaned in and whispered so only she could hear. "Please don't concern yourself with my father. I've got it handled. Tonight is about you. Promise me you'll let it go and enjoy your special night."

She gazed into his eyes. Sincerity shown in their verdant depths and her nerves smoothed out and her heart warmed. This man really did care about her, just as she was falling more and more each day for him. "Deal. I'm just so nervous about all of it. Thank you."

He tilted her chin toward him and pressed a soft kiss on her lips.

The vehicle stopped and Dylan blew out an unsteady exhale. "We're here. Okay everyone, I'm going in now and I'll see you in about half an hour."

Gabriel began to rise as well, but she stopped him with a hand on his firm chest. "No, please let me do this alone. I'll see you with everyone else when the doors open, okay?"

His brows drew together, but he nodded. "Of course. *A bientôt.* See you in a little while."

Dylan scrambled to exit the limousine when the chauffer opened the door. Allowing him to close it behind her, she crossed the sidewalk and tapped on the gallery's closed glass double doors. Adrenaline pumped through her veins and beads of perspiration popped up on her forehead, despite the evening's cool ocean breeze.

Mark O'Day, the gallery director, hurried to the door and waved her inside. "I'm so glad you're early. Everything is ready, but it's always nice for you to have some time to settle into the space before people arrive. Let's check it out and make sure you approve."

Dylan nodded and smiled, like it was everyday her approval was what mattered in an art gallery. Now she knew what people meant by the expression to pinch yourself and make sure you weren't dreaming. Her dream was now reality.

Her legs were shaking and her heart racing in her chest as she perused the display in the front of the gallery. Although she'd negotiated and set prices for each of her paintings, seeing the numbers in black and white beside her name on the wall sent a rush to her brain, like the fizzling of champagne bubbles. Mr. O'Day's words were simply a buzzing in her ears and she nodded and smiled like she was paying attention. She'd done it and without either her father's or Gabriel's mother's assistance.

Her feet tingled to twirl in circles and her hands wanted to pump in the air, but she managed to act professional. She hoped. Whether this would be the first of many showings or the only one, pride filled her. Validation meant something, whether anybody wanted to admit it or not. Especially in the arts where the hope was people would enjoy and purchase your work.

Time began to fly.

Her family and Gabriel entered through the back door of the gallery and joined her. A young waiter appeared with a tray of champagne and her father plucked two glasses off for them. Dylan's heart soared seeing the genuine pride filling her father's handsome face.

Amanda wrapped an arm around her. "Dylan, this is incredible and so deserved. I only wish you'd called the gallery owner a few years ago."

She squeezed her older sister. "I wasn't ready. Tonight feels just right to me."

Suddenly, the two wide rooms of the gallery were brimming with people; a string trio played uplifting classical music, and groups of people clustered around Dylan's paintings. So far nobody had run screaming from the gallery or laughed, so that had to be a good sign.

Michele stepped up and saluted her with her own flute of champagne. "Bravo. I believe you've already sold a few pieces and it's only the first thirty minutes of the evening. I'm very pleased for you." Her elegant features lit up in a smile.

"Merci, Michele. It means so much coming from you."

"I'm also pleased you arranged this show on your own, without even an agent. I believe your career will begin to move rapidly now. In addition to the galleries I'm speaking with, I've also

talked about you to a few agents who would like
to set up interviews. Is that okay?"

Dylan's eyes widened. "Okay? That's fabulous.
Thank you so much. And yes, somehow even if
this the only show I ever have, it's encouraging to
know I did it myself."

"Now you'll have different worries–like if you
have enough paintings for all the places that want
to show your work." Michele's gray eyes sparkled.

"You're teasing me now. And wouldn't I want
to be more exclusive so they have to fight over
me?" Dylan played along with the lovely fantasy.

A strong muscular arm slid around her waist and
Gabriel growled in her ear. "Who do I have to
fight over you? Don't they know you're mine and
I'm not letting you go?"

Dylan gasped, not just at the jolt of heat from
his powerful physique pressed against hers, but
at his words. She recovered quickly–of course he
was playing it up their engagement for everyone,
especially his father. "I'm all yours. Your maman
and I were discussing agents and shows and such."

Gabriel's sculpted mouth spread into a wide grin.
"Of course you were. Your show is a triumph.
Half the paintings have been bid on already."

She frowned at him. "You didn't?"

He shook his head. "No, see, I listen to you. But
I want to. Won't you let me have the one with
the fiery sunset? It reminds me of your beautiful
hair." He stroked his palm down her hair and she
shivered.

"Gabriel. Don't distract her. There's plenty of

time for you two to be alone together after the show." His mother scolded.

His dark brows drew together. "Can't I congratulate my fiancée? And don't worry, Papa wants to talk to me, so I'll have to do that."

He leaned on the cane with the golden carved tiger handle. She'd helped him pick out the cane—if he had to use one, it might as well be fun.

"Shall I come with you?" Michele's delicate winged brows rose and her eyes cooled.

"Non." He shook his head. "Non, he and I need to talk and it may as well be now while Dylan basks in her success. It will only be a few minutes." His jaw grew tight.

"I do need to go mingle and answer questions—I've not done a good job of that yet. But please don't let him ruin the evening." Dylan turned to Gabriel and a slither of unease spread down her spine.

Something about his father's stubborn position about Gabriel returning to France scared her. She didn't want this engagement to end now—no, she wanted every day of their allotted time for their relationship to grow. Her feelings for him deepened by the day. They needed more time together to have a chance to truly fall in love. If his father issued him an ultimatum, would Gabriel break off their relationship and return to France?

"Please don't worry. I've got it handled. I'll be back before you know it." He flashed his straight white teeth and turned to cross the room to where his father stood.

"Please don't concern yourself Dylan. Every-thing will work out." Gabriel's mom's smile was tight as she watched her husband and her son walk toward the back room of the gallery.

"I hope so. Okay, I'll see you in a little while." Dylan smiled, shook her hair back, and sauntered over toward where a group of total complete strangers appeared to be admiring her paintings.

Gabriel wouldn't succumb to his father's demands, would he?

CHAPTER 23

GABRIEL FOLLOWED HIS FATHER THROUGH an open doorway to a small private viewing room. Although there was no actual door, they were away from the majority of the attendees. He'd managed to avoid being alone with his father much since he arrived and didn't appreciate his ambush during Dylan's important night.

"Let's sit." His father gestured to a black velvet couch facing an enormous blank wall where prospective buyers could hang a painting and contemplate it without distraction.

Gabriel sat down and gripped the solid head of his cane until his knuckles turned white. Just in case he'd need to rise quickly and escape. He winced. Patience. Around his father, that quality tended to be in short supply, especially when he expected the same conversation he'd had a thousand times before.

Unwilling to allow his father to dominate the conversation from the outset. "So, Dylan's very talented, isn't she?" Gabriel began.

His father inclined his head. "Oui, actually quite impressive. I understand your mother has been making inquiries for more shows for her. Did Dylan know your mother's reputation when you met?"

Gabriel kept his face impassive. "I'm not sure what you're implying, but they actually began discussing it at the hospital and maman wanted to see the work of her future daughter-in-law right away. Once she did, of course she wanted to help. Why wouldn't she?"

His father shrugged and crossed one lean leg over the other. "Don't be so defensive. Look, let's be frank. There's no need for you to remain in the U.S. Your fiancée can paint and show her work wherever she likes. You are just making excuses and delaying the inevitable."

Gabriel gritted his teeth and spoke slowly. "The point is, I want to make my home here—*we* want to make our home here. Dylan is very close to her family and why should she uproot her life because of your expectations? The McNeills are very close knit, different from our family."

His father shrugged again. "Look, I won't tell you who to marry, but tying the DuVernay name to some Hollywood tabloid name isn't good for our brand. If you two live in Provence, it will be easier to keep the names separate. And if she wants to visit her family, she can use the company jet."

Gabriel's nostrils flared and he sucked in a deep breath. "Bad for our brand? Are you kidding me? You need to wake up and join the rest of the world in the twenty-first century. You've been trying to control my life since the day I was born. And no, you won't tell me how to live the rest of my life. And if you'd open your eyes, you would see the best thing for our brand is Claude."

His father's lips thinned and his blue eyes froze into glacial chips. "You have been gallivanting around the world kicking a ball for your entire adult life. I know better than you possibly could what is good for the brand. My grand-père and my father before me ran the vineyards. You are my son. You've known about this expectation–it's not a surprise. Your football career is finished. So why are you fighting this?"

Gabriel struggled to tamp down the red haze threatening to obscure his vision. "Look. Dylan is one reason I must stay here. My rehabilitation will take at least another few months. You know my passion is football. Since I cannot play any longer, I've been offered opportunities to be a commentator here and help elevate the sport in this country. It's what I want to do. It's what I was born to do."

His father hissed and slammed his glass down on the round metallic table in front of them. "Born to do? How many times do we need to have this discussion? You are a DuVernay and you were born to run our vineyards. You've always known that. I've been patient long enough with your sport because you have—had—true talent."

Gabriel flinched at the past tense and began to reply.

His father held up one hand. "Non. Let me finish and make myself perfectly clear. I am giving you three months, but I expect you back after that, with or without your fiancée. I'm sure you can convince her to join you. If you do not agree, not only will I disown you, but I will make sure—"

"What? Disown me? Why in the world wouldn't you just have Claude take over? She's the right person to run the winery, she's the most talented, and for god's sake, women have been running wineries better than men for years now. I mean, Veuve Cliquot, hello? You're being stubborn and ridiculous."

His father crossed his arms and glared.

Gabriel pushed to his feet and stared down at his father. "I'm tired of you not seeing me and my sister for who we are. Our mother does, and she agrees that Claude should take over the winery and I should do what I love. One thing that impresses me about the McNeills is they love and support their children unconditionally. I don't know why you cannot appreciate my sister and me for who we are."

"Gabriel." His father stood. "The McNeills are some new-money entertainment family—our name goes back generations. Of course your talent has made me proud and Claude is a source of great joy to me. But the bottom line is you need to face that your football life is over and step up to your responsibilities. This engagement is no reason to stay here. And you should be very sure Dylan is not using you to launch her own career."

For a few moments Gabriel couldn't speak. He shook his head. *Enough.* "I will not discuss this with you any longer. You do what you need to do. I love Dylan McNeill and I'm going to spend my life proving that to her every single day. I will follow the path that calls to me and be successful, just as I have done my entire life. If you cannot accept me for who I am, so be it."

His father's jaw dropped. "Gabriel–"

"Non. No more. You've pushed me to make a choice and my choice is Dylan and America. You would be wise to put Claude in charge–research it, having a woman in charge will be good press for the DuVernay name and that seems to be all you value. I'm done."

Gabriel marched out of the room before he yelled any louder. He'd taken two steps out when he caught a glimpse of green and long auburn hair toward the back of the gallery. He hurried as fast as he could with his irregular gait, but was too late. The back door slammed shut behind Dylan. He yanked the heavy metal door wide, but the alley was empty.

She was gone.

Dylan ran down the hill toward the bluff until she stumbled upon the railing overlooking the Pacific. The crisp salty ocean breeze and the dark, star-kissed sky quietly wrapped around her. Tears poured down her cheeks and her breath came in sharp bursts. She wrapped her arms around her waist and squeezed tight, rocking back and forth. How had the best night of her life turned into such a nightmare?

She hadn't meant to eavesdrop when she walked back to the back office to freshen her lipstick and take a lightning-quick break. Her family, friends, and gallery guests were complimentary and full of questions for her. She'd basked in the attention, but needed a moment to catch her breath.

The harsh voices halted her progress and she'd moved quietly to stand against the pale walls by the entrance into the private room. Gabriel and his father's argument sounded nasty. Didier DuVernay seemed like a cold, callous tyrant and when he insulted her family, her temper sparked. Although he wasn't off base regarding Dylan wanting Michele's assistance, nobody disrespected the McNeills. The jerk. And damn it, she'd gotten tonight's show on her own merit. Nobody had helped her.

Her heart shattered for Gabriel when his father scoffed at his appeal for acceptance. Even without seeing his face, his pain translated through his measured words and raised voice. But when he fervently defended her, declared his love for her and desire to spend his life showing her—that's when she broke. Not that she could blame him for laying it on thick, but hearing the words from his lips stabbed into her heart.

It was all an act. An act declaring his independence. An act to convince his father their pretend engagement was real and a viable reason for Gabriel to refuse his father's demands.

How could he have known she'd hear his impassioned speech? How could he have known the moment she heard his beautiful voice claiming he loved her he would destroy her heart?

Because the moment he said he loved her was the moment Dylan recognized the truth she'd been pretending to ignore these past weeks. Each moment they'd spent together had been some of the happiest of her life. Not just their sexual chemistry and easy banter. She admired his strength and his love for his mother and sister, and his sheer dedication to his life's passion. As the layers of his personality unwrapped themselves, she'd fallen deeper and deeper under his spell.

And somehow convinced herself he truly was falling for her. That their six-month bargain would one day become a funny story they might share with their grandchildren. Maybe her family was right—she was a sappy romantic without a realistic bone in her body.

Maybe their over-protectiveness was justified.

Maybe she'd been lying to herself and she'd agreed to their outlandish pretend relationship not for Michele's lofty art world introductions, but because she'd hoped on some level—deep down— he would fall in love with her. For real.

Because she hadn't forgotten their night together in Paris and believed he'd appeared in that nightclub at the exact time she needed a knight in shining armor.

CHAPTER 24

DYLAN PAUSED TO WIPE THE perspiration off her forehead. The Santa Ana winds had kicked in and Rancho Santa Fe was hotter than it had been since last summer's fires. Her studio's enormous skylights, which she loved for the natural light they bestowed, now created more of a greenhouse effect. Despite air-conditioning, it was sweltering. She surveyed the spacious airy room, satisfied with the ruthless organization she'd begun with her paintings. Sam was working on the far side of the room, lending her a hand.

It had been a week since the disastrous finale to her exhibition. Professionally, the evening had been a smashing success, with her selling half of her work on the spot. To real live strangers who she'd never met. For more money than she'd imagined. West Coast Galleries wanted more of her work and she was sorting through canvases to share. A hint of satisfaction filled her. She'd accomplished it all on her own.

That night, once she'd managed to gather her composure, she'd returned to the gallery to find everyone gone except for her family. They'd been frantic because she'd disappeared for more than an hour. Apparently nobody else had overheard Didier and Gabriel's argument, thank goodness.

Michele, always the master negotiator, had stepped in and pled illness, so she and Didier had checked into the nearby Casa Laguna Inn. Gabriel had insisted on taking an Uber to fetch his parents' belongings from Pacific Vista Ranch, so he hadn't been in the gallery when she'd returned. He'd told her family he'd stay with his parents and return the next day once he knew his mom was okay and able to return to France.

Unable to maintain the charade, she'd tucked the breathtaking diamond and emerald heirloom ring into its velvet box, buried beneath layers of gauzy fabric in her t-shirt drawer. She refused to discuss what happened with her family, only telling them she and Gabriel were taking a break. Of course she recognized she'd have to deal with it soon, but she'd been unable to do so.

Her phone beeped. Again. Gabriel had been texting and calling daily, pleading with her to meet with him. She'd ignored the messages and deleted the voicemails. But just like being unable to share with her family, she wasn't emotionally strong enough to face the fact she'd made a gamble and lost. Her heart belonged to Gabriel and he simply wanted freedom.

Why was he being so persistent? What was the point of speaking with him now? He'd stood up to his father and she assumed he was going to take a commentator job and stay in L.A. His dad hadn't really bought the engagement-as-a-reason-to-stay concept anyway. She'd need to see him to say goodbye and have him pick up his belongings. She'd packed them into boxes, which currently resided in the guesthouse laundry room.

But she wasn't quite ready to face him. To look into those bottle green eyes. To acknowledge it was finished. They were finished.

"Dylan, can you come here a second?" Sam called from across the room.

Dylan squared her shoulders and shook off her morose thoughts for now. Work, she'd focus on her work. Living the dream. Ha.

"What's up?" She crossed the room and paused behind her twin.

"Um, what are these?" Sam stood to the side and gestured to a heap of drawings on the floor.

Oh crap. Dylan stared at her sister and quickly dropped her gaze. She held her breath when she saw the pile of sketches. Portrait after portrait of Gabriel. Gabriel in profile like the first times she'd seen him that fateful night in Paris. Gabriel scoring a goal. Gabriel smiling and laughing. No, she didn't look like some online athlete stalker. Not at all.

"Just a few drawings. Nothing." She knelt on the hardwood floor and started gathering the pictures together. "Where did you find these?"

"I picked up one of these portfolios and they slid out. Dylan, look at me."

Dylan sighed and looked up. "Yes?"

"Have you been drawing these since you met

Gabriel last summer?"

She nodded and bit her lip. No more lies.

Sam crouched down next to her and laid a hand on her shoulder. "You love him. Why aren't you taking his calls? What happened the night of your show? Please tell me what's going on."

"I'm going to tell you everything, but you have to swear you won't tell Dad or Angela. Ever." She grasped her twin's hand.

Sam frowned. "Why?"

"Not unless you promise. Okay?" Dylan's stomach clenched and her throat grew dry.

"Of course. You're freaking me out. What is it?" Sam gripped her hand.

Once Dylan began, the words poured out and she couldn't stem the flow. She admitted to not being able to forget Gabriel since their night together in Paris. Her excitement when he'd moved to L.A. and invited her up to his game. Her optimism about them having a chance, even if it started as casual dating.

Her sister's eyes rounded comically when Dylan confessed to the scheme proposed by Gabriel's mother. Sam's jaw clenched when Dylan shared the conversation she'd overheard between Gabriel and his father.

"Oh Dylan, I'm so sorry." Sam bumped her so they were both sitting on the floor and wrapped her arms around her. "What a mess."

They sat for a moment, Dylan absorbing her sister's strength and support. "Yeah."

Sam sat back and grasped her shoulders. "I don't

understand why you aren't talking to him. You said he told his dad he loved you and wanted to spend his life making you happy. So why isn't he here?"

Dylan's eyes filled and she blinked to prevent the tears from falling…again. "Oh, Sam, he didn't mean it. He was just keeping up the act with his dad."

Sam shook her. "You don't believe that. I believe he was telling the truth. Why would he bother continuing to call you multiple times a day if he didn't care? What does he have to gain if he already told his dad he was staying?"

"It's his excuse for his dad, remember?"

"But you said his dad didn't buy it anyway, so that doesn't fly. I think you're doing it again," Sam said.

Dylan frowned. "Doing what again?"

"Running away. I know you hate confrontation, but you ran away to Paris last summer because you didn't want to deal with the situation. I get it. Hell, I wanted to bail too. But I think you're running away from Gabriel because you're scared."

Dylan hesitated. "But I—"

"Love is scary. I get it—Holt turned my world upside down. But the payoff is worth it. Something seemed off when you first told us about him, but the more I saw you two together, the more I could tell you were crazy about each other. And he way he looked at you—wow. He was so proud of you at the gallery, we all noticed. What's the worst that could happen if you hear him out?"

Dylan closed her eyes and drew in a deep breath. Could Sam be right?

She exhaled and looked at her sister. "When did you get so wise? I mean, I am three minutes older than you."

Sam's lips twitched. "I don't know about wise. But we've all dealt with losing mom in different ways. You always seemed like the carefree one with guys, but you've never let anyone in as close as you have with Gabriel. That means you trust him. Couldn't you trust he meant every word he told his dad?"

Dylan nodded. "True. And I guess things couldn't feel much worse right now. I've cried myself to sleep every night and I should be dancing around the ranch because I finally got what I've dreamed of with my art." She bit her lip. "But, what if–?"

Sam shot to her feet, pulling Dylan with her. "Oh come on. Enough. Just call him. No more moping."

A thread of hope shot through her. "Okay, I'll text him. But again, promise me you won't tell."

Sam laughed. "Oh my god–no way. Dad would lose his mind and you'd forever have Angela gazing at you with disappointment when she thought you weren't paying attention. The secret will go to the grave. But you've got to tell Amanda too, okay?"

"I will. I swear, I feel like she suspected. She's so darned observant."

"Right? Jake will never get away with anything." Sam chuckled. "Now text Gabriel or I'll take pictures of all these sketches you did and send them to him. Then he'll know you are crazy about him."

Dylan smiled and fished her phone out of her pocket. Her sister always knew how to make her feel better. "I'll text him right now."

Gabriel propped his leg on the stool next to him and adjusted his tablet on the wide kitchen island. His mother had scheduled a video call with his sister and father to see if they could come to some type of truce. His sister's words from a few weeks ago kept replaying on a loop in his mind. The idea of starting some DuVernay wine production in California would only benefit the family.

And he did love the soil. The vines. The art of making wine.

But none of it would satisfy him without Dylan. After the debacle at her exhibition, Gabriel had stayed in the same hotel as his parents when she'd refused to answer his calls. After a few days of the silent treatment, he'd leased his old condo again on a month-to-month basis because it was still available.

He refused to give up. Now he'd discovered his true feelings for Dylan—his true *love* for Dylan—he'd continue pursuing her, at least until she sat down and discussed everything with him. Everything in the condo reminded him of her; from the sunset view over the ocean to the meals they'd shared right where he was currently sitting. How long would she make him wait and would she give him a chance to express his feelings?

The familiar icon beeped and Gabriel answered the call and his family appeared on screen. "Bonjour."

"Bonjour, Gabriel. You look well. How's the rehabilitation coming along?" His mother asked.

"Still torture, but I'm assured I'm progressing quickly. So." His sister looked calm and his father's expression gave nothing away—an improvement from their last encounter.

"So. We will jump right into our discussion. Let me start and then your father has a few things he wishes to say" His mother gave his dad the side-eye. "Right, Didier?"

"Oui." His father nodded.

Gabriel gestured with one hand for her to continue. His shoulders tensed.

"The three of us have had some serious talks since your father and I returned from California. We've come to some conclusions about the future of our vineyards, but of course you must be included in any final decisions." Michele paused and peered closer into the camera. "Oui?"

He massaged the back of his neck, kneading the taut muscles. "Oui."

His father took over. "First, I would like to apologize." He cleared his throat.

Gabriel straightened in the stool. His father apologize? That would be a first.

"Your mother told me about the…arrangement

you made with Dylan. And also that Claude was involved. It has made me think that perhaps," he hesitated and sighed, "that perhaps I may have been a little stubborn."

Gabriel's eyes widened and he kept his jaw clamped shut with effort.

"A little stubborn, Papa?" Claude rolled her expressive green eyes.

"Claude, let your father speak." His mother interjected.

His father continued, "If my family, my children, even my wife felt the need to deceive me in such a dramatic fashion, then perhaps that means I might be a little unreasonable. Although, I still think you should take over the winery, and not because Claude isn't capable, but because it is our tradition. Are you sure you will stay there?"

Gabriel searched for words. "I don't know what to say. I appreciate your apology. And you owe Dylan an apology as well. I hope her family didn't hear anything you said. Yes, you have been unreasonable. And you haven't really seen Claude or me for who we really are. I am going to stay here. I'm interviewing next week for a commentator position and it is what I want. I hope you will be able to respect my decision."

"Darling, that's wonderful. I'm sure you'll do an incredible job." His mother beamed at him.

"Of course he'll be amazing. And you'll achieve your goal—no pun intended." Claude snickered. "Seriously though—if anyone can help football reach new heights there, it's you."

"Merci." Gabriel's mother and sister were proud–even if his father wasn't.

"You are right I owe Dylan an apology. I was angry. I respect your decision. Although I wish you loved the vines more." His father cleared his throat again before continuing. "But I have always been proud of you. I've never missed a single one of your matches. And I am sorry you can no longer play."

Maybe the screen was reflecting light, but Gabriel would swear his father's eyes looked a little shiny. "Merci. Well, the commentating job isn't the same kind of hours as playing was. I will have some time to do other things as well. Did Claude share with you the conversation we had?"

His mother nodded. "Claude shared with us that you two considered the potential of bringing some cuttings from our vineyards to California and testing out a new branch of DuVernay wines–a small-scale operation. Is this what you mean?"

"Exactly. But first–is it official with Claude?" He'd not had the chance to talk to his sister over the last week.

Claude nodded. "Yes, Papa finally accepts the world is changing and that having a woman be the boss would be good press. Right?" She poked their father's shoulder.

His father nodded, although he wasn't grinning like Claude and his mother. "Yes, you made your point and I agree many flourishing wineries are led by women."

Gabriel's heart lifted. "Who are you and what have you done with my father?"

"Don't push it. I am trying. But I am willing to agree to this experiment with you growing wine there. At least I will know you are valuing your heritage. Will you do this at Dylan's family's ranch?"

And just like that, his mood fell. "I'm not sure about that." No need to share he wasn't sure if Dylan would ever speak with him again.

"Have you two made up yet?" His mother asked.

"She was very upset after hearing our argument. It will all work out." Gabriel shrugged, working to look nonchalant.

He hadn't confided in his mother or sister that he was back in his Manhattan Beach condo. No, he needed to speak with Dylan first.

"Well, if the ranch doesn't work, there is other land you can buy, correct?" Claude asked.

He nodded. "Let's discuss the details later. I need to focus on getting back on my feet and setting up my new job first. Okay?"

His phone buzzed and Dylan's name flashed across his screen. Finally. "Dylan is calling me now, so I will catch up soon. I'm glad everything seems to be on the right track. Au revoir."

He snatched up his phone.

Can we meet tonight? I can drive up to you.

Yes. I'm back in the condo. I will be waiting for you.

Gabriel grinned and smacked his hands down on the counter. Tonight he would open himself up and show Dylan he'd meant every word he'd

told his father about her. She was the most incredible woman in the world and if he had his way,
she'd be his forever.

CHAPTER 25

DYLAN PAUSED IN FRONT OF the condo door, overwhelmed with a sense of déjà vu. The last month had been a whirlwind of seeing Gabriel again, his career ending injury, their bargain, and her first exhibition. Now, here she stood, like none of it had actually happened. Like she'd arrived for one of their first real dates. The glowing sun hung low in the summer sky, the Santa Ana winds sharpened the line of the horizon and promised a dramatic sunset.

Just like when they'd watched it together after his match. Could it really only be a month ago?

But this time, the small velvet box with his grandmother's engagement ring weighed down her turquoise suede satchel. Because they hadn't spoken over the last week, she had no clue if she should hand him the ring right away or if he'd expect her to be wearing it. Perhaps she shouldn't have deleted all his voicemails without listening to them. She pressed her hand against her belly, willing the nerves dancing there to subside.

She squared her shoulders and rang the bell. No more running away. Time to face Gabriel, regard–

less of the outcome.

Dylan ascended the stairs, her pulse accelerating with each step. Bringing her closer to him. No matter if she left here broken-hearted or ecstatic, she'd prove to herself she could face her emotions once and for all. Face Gabriel.

The door whipped open before she could knock. Her breath lodged in her throat.

Gabriel wore all white, the casual t-shirt high-lighting his bronzed skin and chiseled male perfection. Drawstring gray sweatpants hung low on his narrow hips and his tanned feet were bare. Her heart skipped a beat when she met his brilliant green eyes.

"Hi." His husky voice was practically a whisper.

"Hi."

For a moment, she remained on the threshold, her brain refusing to send signals to her feet to enter the condo already. Not awkward at all.

His lips twitched. "Will you please come in?"

Her lips curved up, her pulse now hammering in her temples. "Of course."

She followed him into the main room. The French doors created a perfect frame for the gorgeous tableau of orange sun, golden sand, and azure sea beyond his balcony. Her fingers itched to capture the beauty on canvas, but that painting would probably be committed from memory.

"Can I get you a glass of wine? I just opened some rosé." He crossed to the refrigerator. Two chilled glasses sat on the kitchen island's smooth countertop.

Liquid courage never hurt, especially when she had no idea how to begin this conversation. "Yes please. Is it a DuVernay?"

He poured the wine, the liquid a shade of pale pink, signifying its Provence-style origins, and sank down onto one of the barstools. "Non, sometimes I drink other vintages. This one is from one of the neighboring vineyards–crisp acidity and the slightest hint of tart berry. I think you'll love it."

She sat on the barstool next to him, gripped the wineglass's delicate stem, and sampled the wine. "It's delicious. Thank you." Good grief, would they make small talk all evening? She sniffed the wine to distract herself from his clean masculine scent.

"So. I see you aren't wearing your engagement ring. What have you done with it?"

Dylan exhaled a shaky breath. *Here we go.* "It's in my purse. I wasn't sure what to do with it after... after everything that's happened."

Gabriel's jaw was tight, but she couldn't read the expression in his eyes. "I see. May I have it, please?"

Pain sliced into her heart. Her legs trembled as she rose and picked up her oversized purse. Not trusting herself to speak, she rummaged around in the bag until she finally located the small square box. She wrapped her fingers around it, willing herself to keep her expression calm.

She would not break down in tears. Not now. Not in front of him. Without a word, she placed the box on the countertop and slid it toward him.

He stared at it for a moment, then picked it up and slid it into the pocket of his pants.

She remained standing, unsure if she should leave or say something. But what could she say now? He'd made it clear their pretend engagement was finished with that single request. The shaking in her legs spread throughout her body and she took two steps toward the door. Ready to flee.

"Dylan. Come outside with me. I have some things I must share with you. Please?" He rasped and reached one strong hand out toward her.

She stared at his outstretched hand and closed her eyes for a moment. Follow through. *Hear what he has to say—that's why you came.* She nodded, grabbed her wine, and preceded him out onto the balcony. The salty breeze and the sun's warmth caressed her now icy skin. How could she feel cold when it was unseasonably hot outside?

She sat on one of the cushioned chairs facing the ocean and turned to look at him.

"I didn't tell you how beautiful you look tonight, Dylan. You outshine the setting sun." He gazed intently at her.

"Gabriel, could you please say what you're going to say? We need to clear the air before either of us can move on." Now was not the time for flowery compliments.

"Move on? Is that what you want?" His brows arched.

"Well, you just asked for the ring back." Her heart splintered in her chest.

"Just listen to me, okay?" He waited for her to nod before continuing. "A lot has happened in this last month. Everything has changed. For both of us. When I arrived here in California, all I knew was that I was about to fulfill one of my biggest dreams and I knew I wanted to see you again. I'll be honest, I hadn't really thought beyond that–I only knew I'd never been able to forget you and our night together in Paris. I knew I wanted to see you."

"I hadn't forgotten you either and I was happy when you called. But I agree, I wasn't sure where it would lead or if it would lead anywhere at all. I had to see you too." Her heartbeat accelerated.

"Each time I saw you, I wanted more. I've never experienced that before. But your focus was— is—on your art and mine was on football. I didn't want to see anyone else. I just was focusing on the present."

Dylan nodded. "Me too. But then…" She turned and gazed out toward the deepening sky.

"It's okay to say it. Then my knee blew apart. I'm coming to terms with it. It isn't easy, but I cannot change it." He scrubbed his hands through his chestnut brown hair and sighed.

"I'm so sorry, Gabriel. I wish there was some-thing I could do." She heart warmed at his positive attitude. If she could no longer paint, she wasn't sure she could be so pragmatic.

"You've already done more than most people would consider doing." He shifted forward in his seat, his gaze honing in on hers.

She swallowed, her throat suddenly dry. "Oh, I don't know about that."

"No, nobody would have agreed to my mother's scheme unless maybe they did it for money or fame. No, you took a risk because your heart is compassionate and because you are kind." He threw up his hands. "My god, I got much more out of the bargain, in the end, you didn't even need my mother's help. But you gave me some space when I was at my lowest point. Some space to breathe."

"Gabriel, you make me sound like some saint. I wasn't being selfless. We both benefitted." Her pulse continued to thrum in her veins, but her skin began to thaw.

He shrugged. "Anyway. I will never forget it nor be able to thank you enough. You were there for me when I needed help. You pretended with your family and for that I am sorry. I know how close you are to them and how tough it was for you."

Dylan's shoulders drooped. Admiration and gratitude were one thing, but he'd not mentioned any deeper emotions. "You helped me too. You believed in me. And your mother is introducing me to a few agents she thinks will be a good fit. So I'm not walking away empty handed." She gazed down at her feet, unwilling to meet his gaze.

"Dylan." He scooted the chair forward, the metal legs scraping against the balcony. "Look at me."

She lifted her face toward him and sucked in a

breath at the heat in his emerald eyes. He grasped her hands in his, holding her tight. Her skin tingled where they were connected, and her breath grew shallow.

"The rational thing for us to do now is start over. For us to go back and date like a normal couple. Take our time. Right?"

Dylan's breath hitched. "Date?" How could they go back to dating?

"It's the logical thing. Get to know each other better. Blah, blah, blah. But what I feel for you defies logic. Is anything but normal."

He squeezed her hands tight, then released them and reached into his pocket and whipped out the velvet box.

Dylan held her breath, hope rising in her chest.

"I cannot get down on one knee tonight, but one day I will. Dylan Marie McNeill, I love you more than anything in this world. You make every moment worth living. I learned the hard way that there are no guarantees in this world. I cannot promise to be perfect and I cannot promise what will happen every day, but I can promise to love you with all my heart and treat you with the love and respect you deserve. Will you marry me?"

Dylan half-cried, half-laughed. "You love me?"

"Of course I love you. How could I not love you? But how do you feel about me?" His bottle green eyes gleamed bright.

"I love you. I think I've loved you from the moment we met. I came up here to tell you my feelings. I had no idea if you loved me too." Heat radiated through her.

"Everything I told my father was the truth. You are the only woman for me. Please spend the rest of your life with me so I can show you every day how much." He flicked open the box and offered it to her.

She stared at the sparkling ring–the symbol of his heritage and his commitment. This time, the token offered with love instead of necessity. "Yes. Yes, I will marry you, Gabriel Rene DuVernay."

He grinned and took the ring out, sliding it onto her finger. "I love you. Forever."

Tears of joy streamed down her face. "I love you forever."

He pulled her onto his lap and she wove her arms around his neck, sliding her fingers into his soft hair. "I can't believe this is actually real."

He lowered his head to hers, capturing her lips in a deep kiss. A rush of heat shot through her veins and her heart melted.

After a few satisfying minutes, he murmured against her lips. "Oh, it's real. I'm not letting you go. And I have one more proposal for you."

She nestled in closer to him. "More? I already said yes."

"Well, I don't want to wait. We cannot go to Paris right now to relive our first meeting. But what if we got in your car and drove to Paris in Las Vegas and get married tomorrow?"

She gasped. "Elope? Tomorrow?"

"I know you are the one. Why do we need

to start being traditional now? Let's get married now, just you and me. We can do something with our families later, but I want to prove to you this is real."

Dylan grinned. "So now I can say I'm running away, but running away to get married, not running away from something."

"Run away with me. Run toward our future." Gabriel's eyes pleaded with her to agree.

"Yes. Absolutely yes." She slid her hands up to frame his square-jawed face and pressed her lips to his.

They remained out on the patio, wrapped in each other's arms, until the sun dropped behind the horizon, streaking the sky with brilliant red and violet. A perfect beginning to forever.

EPILOGUE

Six months later

DYLAN AND GABRIEL CANTERED ACROSS the gently sloping green hills toward Pacific Vista Ranch's main house. After one more visit to the far west end of the ranch, where the hills were steeper and the sun the brightest, it was time for a McNeill family meeting. The late morning winter sunshine bathed the pastures with a mellow golden glow and the mild breeze kissed Dylan's skin. Contentment filled her.

"So, you're happy with the land? Are you sure you want to start the vineyard here instead of the other parcel we found?" Dylan glanced at her husband, who looked gorgeous riding Ace, the dapple-grey gelding she'd given him as a wedding present.

Gabriel nodded with a grin. "Oui. I love the idea of combining our families this way. Now that we won't be living on the ranch anymore, it will ensure we are here frequently."

After they'd eloped to Las Vegas, Gabriel revealed more about his desire to plant DuVernay vines in Rancho Santa Fe. Both the DuVernays and the McNeills loved the idea of expansion to California. The new production satisfied Didier's desire for his son to keep a hand in the family business and fulfilled Gabriel's decision to be a vintner on his own terms. When his sister Claude flew over to assess the potential, she wholeheartedly recommended a vineyard on Pacific Vista Ranch.

"I'm so glad. I know my family loves the idea. And you're right, even though our new house is only a few miles away, we'll always have a reason to be here." She'd never lived away from the ranch, except for art school.

They reached the stable, dismounted, and handed the reins to Charlie, one of the grooms. Usually, they'd put the horses away themselves, but the family was waiting at the kitchen table to hear their final decision.

Hand in hand, they sauntered to the main house. Dylan savored the warm strength of Gabriel's long fingers intertwined with hers. Upon entering, the voices from the kitchen were audible from the hallway. When they reached the kitchen, everyone looked up in anticipation.

"Come on in and sit down. We were just laying bets about your decision." Sam laughed and waived a fistful of dollar bills. "I know I'm going to win because I always know what my twin sister wants most."

Gabriel chuckled. "Well, I hope you all bet on us because we'd love to plant DuVernay vines on

Pacific Vista Ranch."

Sam and Holt cheered. "Told you so. Give me your money." She held her hand out to Amanda and Jake, who reluctantly forked over two dollars.

"I can't believe you guys thought we'd decide against the ranch," Dylan said.

Amanda shrugged with a smile. "I didn't, but couldn't let Sam be too smug."

"Hey!" Sam frowned.

"You guys are too funny. It'll be the best of both worlds. And we're only going to be living in Solana Beach—it's not like we'll be living in L.A. or France." Dylan grinned.

She and Gabriel sat down and picked up two flutes of champagne. It was happy hour in France, right?

Chris lifted his glass. "Here's a toast to new beginnings. Gabriel, we're thrilled to have you in the family and excited for our very own wine. Congratulations." Everyone toasted together.

"So this means I get to move back into the guesthouse?" Grant asked. He smiled, but his eyes were guarded.

In a moment where the McNeills were flourishing, their stepbrother was in the midst of a prolonged separation from his wife. Dylan's heart ached for Grant, who was one of the best guys she knew. Hopefully everything would work out for him.

"Yes, you get to have the guesthouse back. We'll be moving next month." She and Gabriel had found a unique property near the bluffs in

Solana Beach where they could share romantic sunsets from their balcony every night.

Gabriel had accepted the part-time position with ESPN and was thriving in his role promoting his beloved sport. By a stroke of luck, he walked with barely a hint of a limp, and was adjusting to talking about soccer instead of playing it. He fit in with the McNeills like he'd been born to the clan.

Dylan's third exhibition started next month in New York and one was in the works in Paris, thanks to Michele's introductions and the success of her first solo show. She grinned as she looked around the table. What began as an escapist evening in Paris had transformed into a life beyond her wildest dreams.

THE END

OTHER BOOKS BY

THANK YOU FOR READING *For The Love of You*! I hope you loved Dylan and Gabriel's story as much as I loved writing it. The next book in the Pacific Vista Ranch series will be a short story featuring Rafe, Jake Cruz's brother and will be part of the Jingle Ball Anthology.

Stay tuned for the next full-length novel in the series, coming in 2020, featuring Grant Michaels, Sam, Amanda, and Dylan's stepbrother. *www. clairemarti.com/mybooks.html*

To find out about new books, book signings and events, and receive exclusive giveaways and sneak peeks of future books, sign up for my newsletter: *www.clairemarti.com*

If you love steamy beach romances, check out my award winning Finding Forever in Laguna series. You'll find previews of *Second Chance in Laguna*, *At Last in Laguna*, and *Sunset in Laguna* here: *www.clairemarti.com/mybooks.html*

And if you have a moment, please leave a review for *For The Love of You* on your favorite book site.

AUTHOR BIO

CLAIRE MARTI STARTED WRITING STORIES as soon as she was old enough to pick up pencil and paper. After graduating from the University of Virginia with a BA in English Literature, Claire was sidetracked by other careers, including practicing law, selling software for legal publishers, and managing a non-profit animal rescue for a Hollywood actress.

Finally, Claire followed her heart and now focuses on two of her true passions: writing romance and teaching yoga. She lives in San Diego with her husband and furry kids.

Made in the USA
San Bernardino, CA
20 March 2020